His Lips Were Only Millimeters From Hers. Already He Could Feel Her Breath Against Him.

"Alex, wait!"

He drew in a shuddering breath, constraining his desire.

"Don't worry, Loren. I will make tonight one you will never forget."

"No, it's not that," she said, pulling out of his arms. "It's about us. Our marriage."

"Us?"

What was she talking about? They were married. Tonight would see the consummation of that marriage.

"Yes, Alex, us. I love you. I've always loved you one way or another. And even knowing you don't love me, I agreed to marry you in part because of my feelings for you, but also to honor my father, and his promise to yours." Her eyes glistened in the candlelight with unshed tears. "Can you honestly tell me that you have done the same?"

Dear Reader,

When this trilogy first started to grow in my mind I really let my imagination wander. Initially this was going to be a royal trilogy, because doesn't everyone love a royal? Well, after a little gentle guidance from my editor at the time, I was persuaded away from the over-the-top fairy-tale aspects of the stories I'd initially outlined and my mind spun off on another tangent. A wealthy family bound by a 300-year-old legend and a curse, and living on a totally fictional Mediterranean island called Isla Sagrado. Just goes to show that all those years of daydreaming in class (and my school reports will support this) were worthwhile after all.

So here we have it. Book #1 of WED AT ANY PRICE—Alexander and Loren's story. My working title for this was *The Spaniard's Honor Bride,* which kept me focused on the deep sense of honor Alex has in his duty to the people of his country and to his family. Of course, his bride was a girl promised to him virtually from the cradle and who has loved him her whole life. The challenge of bringing them together and *keeping* them together was great grist for this writer's mill.

I hope you enjoy *Honor-Bound Groom* and that you look forward to the next instalment in the trilogy, *Stand-In Bride's Seduction,* where Alex's brother, Reynard, meets his match and learns that love is not all about appearances.

Happy reading and very best wishes,

Yvonne Lindsay

YVONNE LINDSAY

HONOR-BOUND GROOM

Published by Silhouette Books
America's Publisher of Contemporary Romance

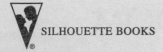 SILHOUETTE BOOKS

ISBN-13: 978-0-373-73042-1

HONOR-BOUND GROOM

Recycling programs for this product may not exist in your area.

Visit Silhouette Books at www.eHarlequin.com

Printed in U.S.A.

Books by Yvonne Lindsay

Silhouette Desire

The Boss's Christmas Seduction #1758
The CEO's Contract Bride #1776
The Tycoon's Hidden Heir #1788
Rossellini's Revenge Affair #1811
Tycoon's Valentine Vendetta #1854
Jealousy & a Jewelled Proposition #1873
Claiming His Runaway Bride #1890
†*Convenient Marriage, Inconvenient Husband* #1923
†*Secret Baby, Public Affair* #1930
†*Pretend Mistress, Bona Fide Boss* #1937
Defiant Mistress, Ruthless Millionaire #1986
**Honor-Bound Groom* #2029

*New Zealand Knights
†Rogue Diamonds
**Wed at Any Price

YVONNE LINDSAY

New Zealand-born to Dutch immigrant parents, Yvonne Lindsay became an avid romance reader at the age of thirteen. Now, married to her "blind date" and with two surprisingly amenable teenagers, she remains a firm believer in the power of romance. Yvonne feels privileged to be able to bring to her readers the stories of her heart. In her spare time, when not writing, she can be found with her nose firmly in a book, reliving the power of love in all walks of life. She can be contacted via her Web site, www.yvonnelindsay.com.

This book is dedicated to all my wonderful readers, who make it possible for me to keep writing books. Thank you from the bottom of my heart.

Prologue

Isla Sagrado, three months ago...

"**A***buelo* is losing his marbles. He talked again of the curse today."

Alexander del Castillo leaned back in the deep and comfortable dark leather chair and gave his brother, Reynard, a chastising look.

"Our grandfather is not going mad, he is merely growing old. And he worries—for all of us." Alex's gaze encompassed his youngest brother, Benedict, also. "We have to do something about it—something drastic—and soon. This negative publicity about the curse is not just affecting him, it's affecting business, too."

"That's true. Revenue at the winery is down this quarter. More than anticipated," Benedict agreed, reaching for his glass of del Castillo Tempranillo and taking a sip. "It certainly isn't the quality of the wine that's doing it, if I say so myself."

"Put your ego back where it belongs and focus, would you?" Alex growled. "This is serious. Reynard, you're our head of publicity, what can we do for the family as a whole that will see talk about this stupid curse laid to rest once and for all?"

Reynard cast him a look of disbelief. "You actually want to lend credence to the curse?"

"If it means we can get things on an even keel again. We owe it to *Abuelo,* if not to ourselves. If we'd been more traditional in our ways then the issue would probably not have arisen."

"The del Castillos have never been renowned for their traditional outlook, *mi hermano,*" Reynard pointed out with a deprecating grin.

"And look where that has put us," Alex argued. "Three hundred years and the governess's curse would still appear to be upon us. Whether you believe in it or not, according to the legend, we're it—the last generation. If we don't get things right, the entire nation—including our grandfather—believes it will be the end of the del Castillo family. Do you want that on your conscience?" He stared his younger brother down before flicking his gaze to Benedict. "Do you?"

Reynard shook his head slightly, as if in disbelief. He seemed stunned that his eldest brother had joined their grandfather in the crazy belief that an age-old legend could be based in truth. And more, that it could be responsible for affecting their prosperity, indeed, threatening their very lives today.

Alex understood Reynard's skepticism. But what choice did they have? As long as the locals believed in the curse, bad publicity would affect the way the del Castillo family could do business. And as long as *Abuelo* believed, the paths he and his brothers chose could make or break the happiness of the man who had raised them all.

"No, Alex." Reynard sighed. "I do not want to be responsible for our family's demise any more than you do."

"So what do we do about it?" Benedict challenged with a humorless laugh. "It's not as if we can suddenly drum up loving brides so we can marry and live happily ever after."

"That's it!" Reynard declared with a shouted laugh and pushed himself up and out of his seat.

His abrupt movement and shout unsettled the dogs sleeping in front of the fire, sending them barking around his feet. A clipped command from Alex made them slink back to their rug and assume their drowsing state.

"That's what we need to do. It'll be a publicity exercise such as Isla Sagrado has never seen before."

"And you think *Abuelo* is losing his marbles?" Benedict asked and took another sip of his wine.

"No," Alex said, excitement beginning to build in his chest. "He's right. That's exactly what we must do. Remember the curse. If the ninth generation does not live by our family motto of honor, truth and love, in life and in marriage, the del Castillo name will die out forever. If we each marry and have families, well, for a start that will show the curse for the falsehood it is. People will put their trust in our name again rather than in fear and superstition."

Reynard sat back down. "You're serious," he said flatly.

"Never more so," Alex answered.

Whether he'd been kidding around or not, Reynard had hit on the very thing that would not only settle their grandfather's concerns but would be a massive boost to the del Castillo name. Its ongoing effect on the people of Isla Sagrado would increase prosperity across the entire island nation.

While Isla Sagrado was a minor republic in the Mediterranean, the del Castillo family had long held a large amount of influence on the island's affairs, whether commercial or political. As the family had prospered so, by natural process, did the people of Isla Sagrado.

Unfortunately, the reverse was also true.

"You expect each of us to simply marry the right women and start families and then, hey, presto, all will be well?" Reynard's voice was saturated with disbelief.

"Exactly. How hard can it be?" Alex got up and patted him on the shoulder. "You're a good-looking guy. I'm sure you have plenty of candidates."

Benedict snorted. "Not the kind he'd bring home to *Abuelo,* I'd wager."

"You can talk," Reynard retorted. "You're too busy racing that new Aston Martin of yours along the cliff road to slow down long enough for a woman to catch you."

Alex walked over to the fireplace and leaned against the massive stone mantel that framed it. Carved from island rock, the hearth had seen generation after generation of his family sprawl in front of its warmth. He and his brothers would not be the last to do so. Not if he had anything to do with it.

"All joking aside, are you willing to at least try?" he asked, his eyes flicking from one brother to the next.

Of the two, Benedict looked most like him. In fact some days he felt as if he was looking into a mirror when he saw his brother's black hair and black-brown eyes. Reynard took after their French mother. Finer featured, perhaps more dramatic with his dark coloring because of it. Female attention had never been an issue for any of them, even from before they'd hit puberty. In fact, with only three years in total separating the brothers, they'd been pretty darn competitive in their playboy bachelorhood. They were all in their early thirties now and had mostly left that phase behind but the reputation still lingered, and it was that very lifestyle that had brought them to this current conundrum.

"It's all right for you, you're already engaged to your childhood sweetheart," Benedict teased him with a smirk, clearly still not prepared to take the matter seriously on any level.

"Hardly my sweetheart since she was only a baby when we were betrothed."

Twenty-five years ago their father had saved his best friend, Francois Dubois, from drowning after the latter had accepted a dare from their father to swim off Isla Sagrado's most dangerous beach below the castillo. In gratitude, Dubois had promised the hand of his infant daughter, Loren, to Raphael del Castillo's eldest son. In a modern society no one but the two men had ever really given any credence to the pledge. But the two men were old-school all the way back down their ancestral lines and they'd taken the matter very seriously indeed.

Alex had barely paid any attention at the time, despite the fact that, virtually from the day she could walk, Loren had followed him around like a faithful puppy. He'd been grateful when her parents had divorced and her mother had taken her away to New Zealand, clear on the other side of the world, when Loren had been fifteen. Twenty-three years old at the time, he'd found it unsettling to have a gangling, underdeveloped teenager telling his girlfriends that she was his fiancée.

Since then, the engagement had been a convenient excuse to avoid the state of matrimony. Until now, he hadn't even considered marriage, and certainly not in the context of Francois Dubois's promise to Raphael del Castillo. But what better way to continue to uphold his family's honor and position on Isla Sagrado than to fulfill the terms of the spoken contract between two best friends? He could see the headlines already. It would be a media coup that would not only benefit the del Castillo business empire, but the whole of Isla Sagrado, as well.

He thought briefly of the dalliance he'd begun with his personal assistant. He didn't normally choose to mix business with pleasure, especially from within his own immediate work environment. But Giselle's persistent attempts to seduce him had been entertaining and—once he'd given in—very satisfying.

A curvaceous blonde, Giselle enjoyed being escorted to the high spots of Sagradan society and entertainment. Certainly she was beautiful and talented—in more ways than one—but wife material? No. They'd both known that nothing long-term would ever have come of their relationship. No doubt she'd be philosophical and he knew she was sophisticated enough to accept his explanation that their intimacy could no longer continue. In fact, he'd put a stop to it right away. He needed to create some emotional space between now and when he brought Loren back to be his bride.

Alex made a mental note to source a particularly lovely piece of jewelry to placate Giselle and turned his mind back to the only current viable option for the position of his wife.

Loren Dubois.

She was from one of the oldest families here on Isla Sagrado, and had always taken great pride in her heritage. Even though she'd been gone for ten years, he'd wager she was still Sagradan to her marrow—and as devoted to her father's memory as she had been to the man during his lifetime. She wouldn't hesitate to honor the commitment made all those years ago. What's more, she'd understand what it meant to be a del Castillo bride, together with what that responsibility involved. And she would now be at the right age, and maturity, to marry and to help put the governess's curse to rest once and for all.

Alex smirked at his brothers. "So, that's me settled. What are you two going to do?"

"You have to be kidding us, right?" Benedict looked askance at Alex, as if he'd suddenly announced his intention to enter a monastery. "Lanky little Loren Dubois?"

"Maybe she's changed." Alex shrugged. It mattered little how she looked. Marrying her was his duty—his desires weren't relevant. With any luck she'd be pregnant with his child within the first year of their marriage and too busy thereafter with the baby to put any real demands upon him.

"But still, why would you choose her when you could have any woman alive as your wife?" Reynard entered the fray.

Alex sighed. Between them his brothers were as tenacious as a pair of wolves after a wounded beast.

"Why not? Marrying her will serve multiple purposes. Not only will it honor an agreement made between our late father and his friend, but it will also help relieve *Abuelo's* concerns. And that's not even mentioning what it will do for our public image. Let's face it. The media will lap it up, especially if you leak the original betrothal story as an appetizer. They'll make it read like a fairy tale."

"And what of *Abuelo's* concerns about the next generation?" Reynard asked, one eyebrow raised. "Do you think your bride will be so happy to ensure our longevity? For all you know she may already be married."

"She's not."

"And you know this because?"

"*Abuelo* had an investigator keep tabs on her after Francois died. Since his stroke last year, the reports have come to me."

"So you're serious about it then. You're really going to go through with a twenty-five-year-old engagement to a woman you don't even know anymore."

"I have to, unless you have any better suggestions. Rey?"

Reynard shook his head. A short sharp movement of his head that bore witness to the frustration they all felt at the position they were in.

"And you, Ben? Anything you can think of that will save our name and our fortunes, not to mention make *Abuelo's* final years with us happier ones?"

"You know there is nothing else," Benedict replied, resignation to their combined fates painting stark lines on his face.

"Then, my brothers, I'd like to propose a toast. To each of us and to the future del Castillo brides."

One

New Zealand, now…

"I have come to discuss the terms of our fathers' agreement. It is time we marry."

From the second his sleek gray Eurocopter had landed on the helipad close to the house she'd wondered what had brought Alexander del Castillo here. Now she knew. She could hardly believe it.

Loren Dubois studied the tall near stranger commanding the space of her mother's formal sitting room. Her eyes drank in the sight of him after so long. Dressed all in black, his dark hair pushed back from his forehead and his brown-black eyes fixed firmly on her face, he should have been intimidating but instead she wondered whether she'd conjured up an age-old dream.

Marry? Her heart jumped erratically in her chest and she tried to force it back to its usual slow and steady rhythm. Years ago, she'd have leaped at the opportunity, but now? With age had come caution. She wasn't a love-struck teenager anymore. She'd seen firsthand what an unhappy alliance could do to a couple, as her parents' tempestuous marriage had attested. She and Alexander del Castillo didn't even know one another anymore. Yet, for some reason, the way he'd proposed marriage—in typical autocratic del Castillo fashion—made her go weak at the knees.

She gave herself a swift reality check. Who was she kidding? He hadn't proposed. He'd flat out told her, as if there was no question that she'd accept. It didn't help that every fiber in her body wanted to do just that.

Wait, she reminded herself. *Slow down.*

It had been ten years since she'd laid eyes on him. Ten years since her fifteen-year-old heart had been broken and she'd been dragged to New Zealand by her mother after the divorce. A long time not to hear from someone by any standards, let alone from the man she had been betrothed to from the cradle.

Even so, a part of her still wanted to leap at the suggestion. Loren took a steadying breath. Although their engagement had always been the stuff of fairy tales, she was determined to stay firmly rooted in the present.

"Marry?" she responded, drawing her chin up slightly as if it could give her that extra height and lessen Alex's dominance over her. "You arrive here with no prior warning—in fact, no contact at all since I left Isla Sagrado—and the first thing you say to me is that it's time we marry? That's a little precipitate, wouldn't you say?"

"Our betrothal has stood for a quarter of a century. I would say our marriage is past due."

There it was—that delicious hint of accent in his voice, characteristic of the Spanish-Franco blend of nationalities of their home country, Isla Sagrado. It was an accent she'd long since diluted with her time in New Zealand, yet from his lips the sound was like velvet stroking bare skin. Her body responded to the timbre of it even as she fought down the wave of longing that spiraled from her core. Had she missed him that much?

Of course she had. That much and more. But she was grown-up now. A woman, not a child, nor a displaced bratty teen. Loren attempted to inject a fine thread of steel into her voice.

"A betrothal that no one seriously expected to be fulfilled, surely."

Somehow she had to show him she wouldn't be such a pushover. In all the time since she'd left Isla Sagrado he'd made no contact whatsoever. Not so much as a card at Christmas or her birthday. His indifference had hurt.

"Are you saying that your father made such a gesture lightly when he offered your hand?"

Loren laughed, the sound of it hollow even to her ears. She still missed her father with a physical ache, even though he'd been dead these past seven years. With him had gone her last link to Isla Sagrado and, she'd believed, to Alex. But now Alex was very much here and she didn't know how to react. *Stay strong,* she told herself. *Above all, stay strong. That's the only way to earn the respect of a del Castillo.*

"A hand that was little more than three months old when it was promised to you—you yourself were only eight," she said with as much bravado as she could muster.

Alex moved a step toward her. She almost felt the air part to allow him passage; he had that kind of presence. Despite her inexperience with men of Alex's caliber, it was one she responded to instinctively.

Alex had always been magnetic, but the past ten years had seen a new maturity settle on his broad shoulders, together with a stronger and more determined line to his jaw. He looked older than the thirty-three years she knew him to be. Older and harder. Certainly not a man who took "no" for an answer.

"I'm not eight anymore. And you—" he paused and ran his eyes over her body "—you are most certainly no longer a child."

Loren's skin flared hot, as if he'd touched her with more than a glance. As if his long strong fingers had stroked her face, her throat, her breasts. She felt her nipples tighten and strain against the practical cotton of her bra. And the longing within her grew harder to resist.

"Alex," she said, her voice slightly breathless, "you don't know me anymore. I don't know you. For all you know I'm already married."

"I know you are not."

He knew? What else did he know about her, she wondered. Had he somehow kept tabs on her all this time?

"It would be foolish for us to marry. We don't even know if we're compatible."

"We have the rest of our lives to learn the details of what we can do to please one another."

Alex's voice was a low murmur and his eyes dropped to her mouth. Please or pleasure? Which had he really meant, she thought, as she struggled against the urge to moisten her lips with her tongue. The longing sharpened and drew into a tight coil deep within her. Loren fought back a moan—the pure, visceral response to his mere gaze shocking her with its intensity.

Her lack of experience with men had never bothered her before this moment. All her dealings with guests and male staff here at her mother's family's sheep and cattle station had been platonic and she'd preferred it that way. It had been difficult enough to settle into the isolation of the farm without the complications of a relationship with someone directly involved with the day-to-day workings of the place. Besides, anything else would have felt like a betrayal—to her father's promise and to the lingering feelings she still bore for Alex.

Now, that lack of experience had come back to haunt her. A man like Alex del Castillo would certainly expect more than what she had to offer. Would demand it.

In her younger years, she'd adored Alex with the kind of hero worship that a child had for an attractive older person—and, oh yes, he'd been attractive from the moment he'd drawn his first breath. She'd seen the photos to prove it. She'd believed that adoration had deepened into love, love not dimmed by Alex's vague tolerance of the scrawny kid who followed him like a shadow around the castillo that had been his family home for centuries.

For as long as she could remember she'd plagued her father to repeat the story of how Alex's dad, Raphael, had saved him from drowning on the beach below the castillo after a crazy dare between friends had almost turned deadly. And she'd hung on his every word as he'd reached the part where, in deepest gratitude, he'd promised his newborn daughter in marriage to Raphael's eldest son.

But her childish dreams of happily ever after with

her fairy-tale prince were quite different from the virile, masculine reality of the man in front of her. Every move he made showed that Alex had a degree of sensual knowledge and experience she couldn't even begin to imagine, much less match. It was exciting and intimidating all at once. Was she already in over her head?

"Besides," Alex said, his voice still low, pitched only for her ears, "it is time now that I marry and who better than the woman to whom I've been affianced all her life?"

Alex's dark brown eyes bored into hers, daring her to challenge him. But, surprisingly, beneath the dare, Loren saw something else reflected in their depths.

While he'd appeared so strong and self-assured from the moment he'd alighted from the helicopter and strode toward their sprawling schist rock home nestled near the base of the Southern Alps, there was now a hint of uncertainty in his gaze. As if he expected some resistance from Loren to the idea that they fulfill the bargain struck between two best friends so long ago.

The scent of his cologne wove softly around her like an ancient spell, invading her senses and scrambling her mind. Rational thought flew out the window as he took another step closer to her, as his hand reached for her chin and tilted her face up to his.

His fingers were gentle against her skin. Her breath stopped in her chest. He bent his head, bringing his lips to hers—their pressure warm, tender, coaxing. His hand slid from her jaw to cup the back of her neck.

Loren's head spun as she parted her lips beneath his and tasted the intimacy of his tongue as it gently swept the soft tissue of her lower lip. A groan rippled from her throat and suddenly she was in his arms, her body aligned tightly against the hard planes of his chest, his abdomen. Her arms curved around him, snaking under the fine wool of his jacket and across the silk of his shirt. The heat of his skin through the finely woven fabric seared her hands. She pressed her fingertips firmly into the strong muscles of his back.

She fit into the shape of his body as though she had indeed been born to the role, and as his lips plundered hers, all she could, or wanted to, think of was how it felt to finally be in his arms. Not a single one of her frustrated teenage fantasies had lived up to the reality.

This was more, so much more than she'd ever dreamed. The strength and power of him in her arms was overwhelming and she clung to him with the longing of a lifetime finally given substance. It barely seemed real but the solid presence of him, his skillful mouth, the sensation of his fingertips massaging the base of her scalp, all combined to be very, very real indeed.

Every nerve in her body was alive, gloriously alive, and begging for more. She'd never experienced such a depth of passion with another man and was certain she never would.

She knew to her very soul that this connection, this instant magnetic pull between them, was meant to be forever, just as their fathers had preordained. And, with this one embrace, she knew she wanted it all.

In the distance she heard the front door slam, its heavy wooden thud echoing down the hardwood floor of the main hallway. Reluctantly she loosened her grip and forced herself to draw away from Alex's embrace. The instant she did so, she almost sobbed. The loss of his warmth, his touch, was indescribable. Loren fought free of the sensual fog that infused her mind as her mother swept into the sitting room, the staccato tap of her swift footfall fading into silence as she stepped onto the heirloom Aubusson carpet.

"Loren! Whose is that helicopter out on the pad? Oh!" she said, displeasure twisting her patrician features. "It's you."

It was hardly the kind of welcome Naomi Simpson generally prided herself on, Loren noted with a trace of acerbity. As her mother's gaze darted between her and Alex, Loren fought not to smooth her hair and clothing, drawing instead on every ounce of her mother's training to appear aloof and in control—at least as far as her hammering heartbeat rendered her capable.

Alex remained close at her side, one arm now casually slung about her waist, his fingers gently stroking the top of her hip through her red merino wool sweater. Tiny sizzling tendrils of electricity feathered along her skin at his lazy touch and she found it hard to focus.

Her mother had no such difficulty.

"Loren? Would you care to explain?"

There was no entreaty in Naomi's words. Even phrased as a question she demanded answers and, if the frozen look of fury on her face was any indicator, she wanted those answers right now.

"Mother, you remember Alex del Castillo, don't you?"

"I do. I can't say I ever expected to see you here. I'd hoped we were completely shot of Isla Sagrado the day we left."

With typical Gallic charm Alex nodded toward Naomi. "It is a pleasure to see you again, Madame Dubois."

"I wish I could say the same. And, just for the record,

I go by Simpson now," Naomi answered. "Why are you here?"

"Mother!" Loren protested.

"Don't worry, Loren," Alex murmured into her ear. "I will deal with your mother."

The warmth of his breath against the shell of her ear sent a tiny tremor down her spine. He exaggerated the two syllables of her name, emphasizing the last to give it an exotic resonance totally at odds with her everyday existence here on the station.

"Nobody needs to deal with anyone," she replied. She cast a stern look at Naomi. "Mother, you are forgetting your manners. That is not the way we treat guests here at the Simpson Station."

"Guests are one thing. Ghosts from the past are quite another."

Naomi threw herself into the nearest chair and glared at Alex.

"I'm sorry, Alex, she's not normally so rude," Loren apologized. "Perhaps you should go."

"I think not. There are matters that need to be discussed," Alex answered, his attention firmly on Naomi's bristling presence.

He guided Loren to one of the richly upholstered sofas before settling his long frame at her side. A shiver of awareness rippled through her as his presence imprinted along her body.

"I believe you know why I'm here. It is time for Loren and me to fulfill our fathers' promise to one another."

Naomi's snort was at total odds with her elegant appearance.

"Promise? More like the ramblings of two crazy men who should have known better. No one in the developed world would sanction such an archaic suggestion."

"Archaic or not, I feel bound to honor my father's wish. Much as I imagine Loren does, also."

Loren felt that shiver again as Alex responded to her mother's derision. Naomi wasn't the kind of woman who liked to be contradicted. She ruled the station with an iron fist and a razor-sharp mind and was both respected and feared by her staff. Despite her designer chic wardrobe and her petite frame she was every bit as capable as any one of the staff here. A fact she had proven over and over again. But she was very much accustomed to being in charge, with her decrees accepted without question. The problem was, Alex was used to that, too. This confrontation could get messy, especially once her mother realized whose side Loren was on.

"Loren." Her mother turned to her with a stiff smile on her carefully tinted lips. "Surely you're not going to take this seriously. You have a life here, a job, responsibilities. Why on earth would you even consider this outrageous plan?"

Why indeed, Loren wondered as she looked around her. Yes, she had a life here. A life she'd been dragged to, kicking and screaming and full of sullen teenage pout. She'd never wanted to live with her mother but her father hadn't contested his wife's petition for full custody of their only child. Loren had later realized that had in part been because he'd never believed Naomi would actually go through with the divorce and relocate to the opposite side of the world. But his apparent indifference had hurt at the time and she'd arrived here at the Simpson Station feeling as though her entire world had been ripped apart. With that kind of beginning, it was hardly surprising that she'd learned to accept her place at the station, but she'd never learned to love it.

And as for her work here and her responsibilities? Well, it would only be Naomi who missed her, and then only for as long as it took to browbeat some other assistant into docile submission. No. Loren had nothing to hold her here. She and Naomi had never enjoyed the kind of mother-daughter relationship that Loren knew others had and she had learned very early that it was easier to accede to her mother's wishes than fight for her own. On Isla Sagrado, Loren had been almost solely her father's child, and Loren had always believed her mother had taken her from the island more as a punishment for Francois Dubois than out of any kind of maternal instinct.

She'd missed Isla Sagrado every day of the past ten years. Of course that pain of loss, the wrench of being repatriated, had dimmed a little over time, but it was still as real now as the man seated alongside her.

Seeing him again was as if he'd brought with him the heat and splendor and lush extravagance of Isla Sagrado. Not to mention the promise of the revival of a passion for living that had lain dormant within her since she'd left the country of her birth.

Yes, her initial reaction to Alex's arrival here had been shock and disbelief. But it was clear he meant what he said. Why else would he have traveled half the world to come and see her?

Thoughts spun through her mind with lightning-fast speed. Her earlier objections, as weak as they were, had come reflexively—a direct result of surprise at the manifestation of the man who'd been a part of her dreams her entire life. She'd wanted—no, she'd *needed*—to hear him refute her doubts to her face. To tell her they belonged together as she'd always imagined, as she'd pretty much lost hope of imagining.

Now she knew what it was like to be in his arms, to feel truly alive for the first time she could remember, there was no way she was going to turn her back on her destiny with the only man she'd ever loved.

"Why would I consider marrying Alex? I would have thought that was quite straightforward," Loren responded with as much aplomb as she could muster under her mother's piercing gaze. "Inasmuch as Alex wishes to honor his father, so do I mine. I've always understood that this would be my future, Mother." She turned her face to look at Alex. "And it's what I've always wanted. I would be honored to be Alex's wife."

"How on earth could you know what you want?" Naomi demanded, pushing up out of her chair and pacing back and forth between them. "You've barely been off the station since we've lived here. You haven't experienced the world, other men, anything!"

"Is that what it really takes to make a person happy? Are *you* truly happy?" Loren held her mother's gaze as her questions unerringly hit their mark. Naomi gaped for a moment, clearly surprised to hear Loren fight back. But even Naomi couldn't deny the truth of what Loren had said.

Naomi's affairs were legend in New Zealand—her power and beauty made for a magnetically lethal combination—and yet, even though many had tried, no man had captured her heart. Loren knew she didn't want that life for herself.

"We're not talking about me. We're talking about you—your future, your life. Don't throw it away on a pledge made before you can even remember. You are worth so much more than that, Loren."

Loren felt the walls, her mother's walls, closing in around her and she pushed them back just as hard.

"Exactly, Mother." Loren sat up straighter, confidence coming from Alex's warmth against her side—confidence to speak her mind at last and say the words she'd locked down deep inside for too long. "I stayed here because I had nothing else to do. Growing up on Isla Sagrado, I believed I had a purpose, a direction. When you and Papa split up I lost that. You took me away from the only future I ever wanted."

"You were just a child—"

"Maybe then, yes. But I'm not a child any longer. We both know I've been marking time these past few years. You know my heart isn't in the station like yours is. You always felt displaced on Isla Sagrado. That's how I feel here. I want to go back.

"As you so correctly pointed out, we are talking about *my* future and *my* life—and I want that to be on Isla Sagrado, with Alex."

He could hardly believe it had been so easy. Alex savored the exhilaration that surged within him as Loren's words hung on the air between mother and daughter.

His body continued to throb in reaction to the slightly built woman at his side, remembering how it felt to be pressed against her far more intimately. Yes, kissing her had been a risk, but he'd built his formidable business reputation on taking big risks and reaping even bigger rewards. This had definitely been a risk worth taking.

Just one look at her had been enough to prove the information he'd been given about her sheltered lifestyle. She appeared as untouched and protected as she'd been the day she left Isla Sagrado. But beneath that inexperienced exterior beat a sensual heart. Wakening that side of her would be a delight and would make the whole process of providing *Abuelo* with a great-grandchild, as proof the curse did not exist and laying it to rest once and for all, an absolute pleasure.

Alex tilted his head slightly to watch Loren as her mother began a tirade of reasons why she should not return to Isla Sagrado. He wasn't worried about Naomi's arguments. If there was one thing he remembered most clearly about Loren as a child it was that despite her quiet attitude, there was no matching her tenacity once she had made up her mind. The vast number of his girlfriends she'd scared off being a case in point.

Instead of following the argument, he took the time to fully take in the woman who would be his wife. Her long black hair, scraped back in a utilitarian ponytail, showcased the delicate structure of her face. And what a face—the child's features he remembered had matured into those of a beautiful young woman's. Her brows were still strong and delicately arched but the eyes beneath them, dark brown like his own, glowed with an inner fire, and her lips were full and lush. Fuller, perhaps, because of their recent kiss, and certainly something he wanted to taste and savor again.

Where had that gawky kid who'd followed him around incessantly disappeared to? In place of the slightly older version of her that he'd expected, he'd discovered a woman who, while she had every appearance of fragility and a vulnerable air about her that aroused his protective instincts, somehow had managed to develop a backbone of pure steel.

He was reminded of Audrey Hepburn as he looked at her now. The gamine features, matured into beauty—the delicate bone structure, intensely feminine. Something else roared to life from deep inside of him. Something ancient, almost feral. She was his—betrothed to him as a matter of honor between friends, but his nonetheless. And she'd stay that way. Nothing Naomi could say would ever change that.

TWO

Despite the luxurious trappings of first class, Loren had been unable to sleep during the long journey from New Zealand. After a day and a half of travel and changeovers she felt weary and more than a little disoriented as she made her way through Sagradan customs and immigration. Nothing about the airport was familiar to her anymore. Still, she supposed as she hefted her cases from the luggage carousel and onto a trolley, it was only natural that change had come to Isla Sagrado in the ten years she'd been gone.

Even so, a pang for the old place she'd left behind lodged behind her heart. Loren shook her head. She was being fanciful if she expected to be able to walk back into her old life as if she'd never left. So much had changed. Her father was gone, her mother was now half a world away and here she was—engaged and preparing to reunite with her fiancé of only a few weeks.

It didn't seem real, Loren admitted to herself—and not for the first time. Everything had moved so fast from the moment she'd told her mother she was returning to the home of her birth. Well, at least once Naomi had recognized that she could not sway her only child's stubborn insistence that she would be marrying Alexander del Castillo.

Alex had taken control once her mother had ceased her objections and washed her hands of the matter, smoothing the way toward having Loren's expired Sagradan passport renewed and booking her flights to Isla Sagrado. Loren hadn't had to lift so much as a finger. Well used to taking care of such details for both her mother and for the overseas guests who visited the massive working sheep and cattle station, it had been a pleasure to have someone else take care of her for a change.

Once he'd had everything organized to his satisfaction, Alex had departed, but not before arranging a private dinner for just the two of them, off the station. They'd choppered to Queenstown, where they'd visited a restaurant on the edge of Lake Wakatipu. The late autumn evening had been clear and beautiful and the restaurant every bit as romantic as Loren had ever dreamed.

By the time they'd returned to the station she knew she was totally and irrevocably in love with him. Not the innocent adoration of a child nor the all-absorbing puppy love of an adolescent, but the deeper knowledge that, no matter what, he was her mate in this lifetime and any other.

He'd been solicitous and attentive all night and, before walking her to her small suite of rooms in the main house at the station, he'd kissed her again. Not with the heated, overwhelming rush of emotion that consumed her the day he'd arrived, but with a gentle, sure promise of greater things to come. Her body had quivered in response, eager to discover the depths of his silent promise right there, right then. But Alex had backed off, cupped her cheek with one warm strong hand, and told her he wanted to wait until their wedding night—it would make their union more special, more intimate.

It had only made her love him more and had served to leave her fraught with nerves the entire journey to Isla Sagrado. Nerves that now left her giddy with exhaustion and made battling the broken wheel on her luggage cart all the more taxing. Fighting the way the thing wanted to veer to the left all the time, Loren paid little attention to the sudden silence in the arrival hall as she came through the security doors after clearing customs.

A silence that was suddenly and overwhelmingly broken by the flash of camera bulbs and a barrage of questions flung at her from all directions and in at least three different languages.

One voice broke over all the rest to ask in Spanish, Isla Sagrado's dominant language, "Is it true you're here to marry Alexander del Castillo and break the curse?"

Loren blinked in surprise toward the man, even as a multitude of others around him continued with their own questions.

A movement at her side distracted her from answering. A tall and stunningly beautiful woman, wearing a startling red dress, hooked an arm around her and leaned forward, her long, honey-blond hair brushing Loren's arm like a swathe of silk.

"Don't answer them. Just smile and keep walking.

I'm Giselle, Alex's personal assistant. I'm here to collect you," she murmured in a French-accented voice that was very un-assistantlike. Her emphasis on the word *personal* hinted strongly at things Loren herself had no experience of.

"Alex isn't here?" Loren blinked to fight back the sudden tears that sprang to her eyes as sharp points of disappointment cut through her.

Believing he'd be here to welcome her home at the end of her journey had been what had kept her going these past few hours. Now, she fought to keep her slender shoulders squared and her sagging spine upright. Struggled to keep placing one foot in front of the other.

Giselle put her free hand on the handle of the luggage cart and directed it, and Loren, toward the exit. Airport security had miraculously cleared a path and beckoned them toward the waiting limousine at the curbside.

"If he'd have come, the media circus would have been worse and we'd never have cleared the airport," Giselle said in her husky voice. "Besides, he's a very busy man."

Giselle's intimation that Alex had far more important things to attend to than collecting his fiancée from the airport pierced Loren's weariness, making her stumble slightly.

"Oh, dear," the other woman said, tightening her hold around Loren's waist. "You're a clumsy little thing, aren't you? You'll have to improve on that, you know, or the media are going to have a field day with you."

While Giselle's tone was light, Loren felt the invisible slap of disapproval behind her words. But there was no chance to respond right away. They were at the car at last. There, a uniformed chauffeur, who looked more like a bodyguard than a driver, hefted her cases into the voluminous trunk of the limo as if they weighed little more than matchsticks. Once that was taken care of, Loren took the opportunity to speak.

"I'm tired, that's all. It's been quite a trip," she responded as she slid over onto the broad backseat of the limousine, her voice a little sharp, earning her an equally sharp look from Giselle in return.

"Touchy, too, hmm?" Giselle narrowed her beautiful green eyes and gave Loren an assessing look. "Well, we'll see how you measure up. Since Reynard issued the press release about Alex's engagement, the whole drama of your father's near drowning and him giving you away afterwards has been front-page news. Goodness knows paparazzi will be crawling all over you to find out about you."

"I'm surprised. I thought Alex might have kept that quiet," Loren said, frowning at the thought of having to rehash the story of her and Alex's fathers' actions over and over again.

"Quiet? Hardly. With the way things are here they need all the strong publicity they can get. You must remember how the island's prosperity seems to be intrinsically linked with the del Castillos'. Whether there's any truth to the curse or not, everyone here is lapping up the story. Promises of happily ever after and all that. Honestly, they've made it all sound so sweet it's almost enough to give you cavities." Giselle finished with a high-pitched laugh that didn't quite ring true.

"So you don't believe in happily ever after?"

"Sweetie," Giselle replied with a smile stretching her generous lips into a wide curve of satisfaction, "what's more important is if Alex believes in it. And we both know he's far too pragmatic for that. Besides, it's not like you two are going to have a real marriage."

"Well, I certainly expect we'll have a real marriage. Why else would we even bother?"

"Oh, dear, you mean he hasn't said anything yet?"

Loren felt her already simmering temper begin to flare. "Said anything about what?" she asked through clenched teeth.

"About keeping up appearances, of course. Though perhaps he thought it would be clear. After all, if he'd had any interest in a *real* marriage he'd have wanted to have some say in the organization of the wedding ceremony and reception, wouldn't he? Instead, he gave me carte blanche. But don't you worry, I'll make sure you have a day to remember."

"Well, *I'd* like to go over the wedding details with you later on, when I'm more rested," Loren asserted, pausing for effect. "Then I'll more than happily take the arrangements off your hands. I'm sure you have far more important things to occupy yourself with."

Loren chose to ignore the rest of what the woman had said. She knew she and Alex had little time before their proposed wedding date only two weeks away, but surely he hadn't left everything to his assistant—his *personal* assistant, she corrected herself.

"Oh, but I have everything under control. Besides, Alex has signed off on what I've done already. To change anything now would only cause problems."

The implication that Loren would bear disapproval from Alex for those problems sat very clearly between the two women. Loren took a steadying breath. She wasn't up to this right now but she knew what Giselle was doing. She'd probably taken one look at Loren and totally underestimated her. Clearly Giselle had some kind of bond with Alex that she didn't want to let go. Maybe she'd even harbored a notion of a relationship with him.

Whatever might have happened between Alex and Giselle before she had arrived home, Loren was his fiancée, and she'd prove she was no walkover. Her battle with her mother to come here in the first place had proven to her that she was anything but that.

"Well," she said, injecting a firm note into her voice, "we'll see about that once I've checked everything over and conferred with Alex." At the other woman's sharply indrawn breath she added, "It is *my* wedding, after all."

Loren settled back against the soft leather upholstery and gazed out the window of the speeding limousine, wondering if she had gone too far in establishing where she stood with Giselle. Perhaps she'd been oversensitive, worn out as she was with travel. But underneath Giselle's self-assuredness and apparent solicitude she sensed a vague but definite threat, as if she was stepping where she wasn't fully welcome by coming back to Isla Sagrado.

She stifled a sigh. She'd expected her homecoming to be different, sure, but when push came to shove she couldn't forget what—or more importantly, *who*—had brought her here.

Alex.

Just thinking about him created a swell of longing deep inside. Without thinking, she traced the outline of her lips with her fingertips, silently reliving their last kiss. If she tried hard enough she could still feel the pressure of his mouth against hers, still experience the heady joy of knowing he'd traveled to New Zealand to fulfill their fathers' bargain—that he'd seen her and still wanted *her*.

Loren let her hand drop back into her lap and stared out the passenger window, searching for familiar signposts and buildings. The landscape had changed so much that Isla Sagrado hardly felt like home anymore, she thought sadly as the unfamiliar roads and buildings swept by them.

The soft trill of a cell phone startled Loren from her reveries. From the corner of her eye she saw Giselle lift a phone to her ear.

"Alex!" Giselle answered, her voice warm and sweet as honey.

Loren's stomach clenched in excitement and she waited for Giselle to hand the phone over to her so she could speak with him herself.

"Yes, I have your future bride here in the car. I expect we'll be at the castillo in about half an hour." She cocked her head to one side and smiled as she listened. "Fine. Yes. I'll let her know."

Giselle flipped the phone shut and gave Loren a smile. "Alex sends his apologies but he won't be able to meet with you until this evening. Business, you understand."

If Loren wasn't mistaken, there was a distinct hint of smugness in the other woman's glittering emerald gaze. She swallowed her disappointment. Not for anything would she yield so far as to display even one hint of weakness, no matter how bitter the pill that Alex couldn't spare even a few minutes to greet her on her first day here.

"Of course. I look forward to the opportunity to have a little rest and freshen up before I see him." Loren smiled in return, summoning a bravado she hoped she could pull off. "Besides, Alex and I have the rest of our lives together. What're a few more hours?"

Alex put down his office phone and stared out the window. It looked down and over the sprawling luxury waterfront resort that was his main concern in the management of the del Castillo financial empire. From his position, it looked beautiful and peaceful, but appearances could be deceiving.

A matter between two of his key management staff that he'd thought Giselle had settled weeks ago had flared up again today with no apparent warning. He sighed. There was no accounting for personalities and how people could either rub along together or end up rubbing one another entirely the wrong way. Add to that the constant harping on about the wretched governess's curse, both in the media and in the whispers among the staff—suffice it to say that the sooner this wedding was done and Loren was pregnant with his child, the better.

How a nation of well-educated and forward-thinking people could remain so superstitious defied belief. The legend of the governess and her curse on the del Castillo family when she was spurned by her lover was just that. A legend. There was no proof. Even the media interest he himself had encouraged had turned into a two-headed beast he could barely tolerate. Giselle had been an enormous help, always stepping in to deflect questions away from him so she could handle them herself.

And she had come to his aid again today. In the face of the urgency in dealing with today's debacle, her calm suggestion that she collect Loren from the airport had been welcome. Giselle was a consummate professional.

He knew she'd make Loren feel at home and get her comfortably settled at the castillo.

If he'd gone to get her, the press would never have let them leave. They'd still be there, posing for pictures, answering questions—wasting time that could be better spent letting Loren unwind after her flight and letting Alex get this administrative headache straightened out. It would be much better for Alex to spend time with her tonight, at the quiet family dinner he'd organized with his brothers and his grandfather, and no press around to badger them.

He allowed himself a small smile at the thought of his grandfather's excitement over their planned dinner. *Abuelo's* reaction when told that Loren would be returning to Isla Sagrado as his future bride had been worth the time away from the problems at the resort to visit with her.

He thought back to when he'd broken his brief liaison with Giselle. She'd pouted a little but had taken his decision, and the diamond tennis bracelet he'd bought her as a severance gift, with good grace and assured him her efficiency in her work would continue. And she'd reiterated her willingness to take up where they'd left off should he ever change his mind.

Until he'd seen Loren again, he'd given Giselle's offer some serious thought. After all, once he'd married and met *Abuelo's* concerns by ensuring the next del Castillo generation would be born, why shouldn't he have some fun? But, despite the clinical manner in which he'd imagined this alliance would go forth, from the second his lips had touched Loren's there had been something about her that had pushed Giselle's offer right out of his mind.

That Loren was unschooled in the ways of love was

clear, but how unschooled? The thought that she might be a virgin both intrigued and enticed him. To be her first lover, to unlock the sensual creature he'd tasted in that first kiss? Oh yes, there were definitely aspects of his marriage to Loren Dubois that he found himself looking forward to far more than he'd anticipated. Now, if he was going to enjoy any time with Loren later today he needed to catch up with his work here at the resort. Fortunes didn't make themselves—legend or no.

By the time Giselle returned to the office he was entrenched in his work. He lifted his head only briefly when she came in with some papers.

"I hope Loren didn't mind I couldn't be there to greet her. Is she all settled now at the castillo?" he asked, scoring his signature across the letters she leaned over to place on his desk.

"Of course she minded you weren't there. Wouldn't any woman?"

Giselle laughed, but he noticed her smile did not quite reach her eyes.

Her fragrance, as heady and sensual as the woman herself, wove around him. But rather than the usual reaction it evoked in him—an anticipation of pleasurable things to come—he was reminded instead of the contrast between his assistant's overt sexuality and Loren's more subtle blend of allure. For some perverse reason, the latter was now far more appealing.

"And yes, in answer to your question, I made sure she was completely comfortable in her suite," Giselle answered. "Although she did seem very weary from her travel."

"Too tired for the dinner with *Abuelo* tonight, do you think?"

"Well, obviously I can't speak for her but, yes, she

did look rather shattered. I wouldn't be at all surprised if she slept all the way through until morning."

Alex furrowed his brow in a frown. Until morning? That wouldn't do. *Abuelo* was looking forward to renewing his acquaintance with the daughter of the man who'd been his son's best friend for so many years. An edge of irritation slid under his skin at the thought that Loren would prefer to sleep rather than spend the evening with him. Alex had planned to present her with the del Castillo betrothal ring tonight. The official seal of their engagement. He huffed out a breath.

"Well, she's just going to have to find her strength from somewhere. The dinner is far too important to postpone."

He missed the subtle curve of Giselle's mouth as he voiced his frustration.

"She probably will benefit from a few good meals, Alex. She does look rather…frail," Giselle commented as she collected the papers off his desk and turned to go back to her desk in the outer office.

"Frail?"

Alex frowned again. Certainly Loren was very slightly built, but in his arms he'd felt the strength and suppleness of her body. Plus, he'd witnessed firsthand her mental determination.

"Appearances can be deceptive," he concluded. "She will be fine, I'm sure."

"Would you like me to make sure she's ready for the dinner tonight?"

"No, Giselle, that won't be necessary, but thank you."

"No problem." His assistant smiled in return before closing his door behind her.

Alex sat staring at the door for some time, comparing

the disparities between the two women. Aside from the obvious physical differences—Giselle's lush femininity versus Loren's more gamine appearance—they were worlds apart in other matters. While Giselle tended to be exactly what she appeared to be, and wasn't afraid to say exactly what she wanted, Loren had hidden strengths. The way she'd dealt with her mother's objections being a case in point. The phrase "still waters run deep" had been designed with someone like Loren in mind, he was sure.

Had he done the right thing? He pinched the bridge of his nose in an attempt to alleviate the throbbing headache that had begun behind his eyes. He had to have made the right choice. To have done anything else was unacceptable. Loren had all the credentials—from her bloodlines right down to her experience within the milieu where he moved socially. This marriage between them *would* work. She was everything he needed in a wife and he would do whatever he had to in order to be what she needed in a husband.

The late-afternoon sun slanted like a blush of color across the golden brick of the castillo as he approached. A wry smile tweaked at Alex's lips as he realized just how much he took for granted that the medieval stronghold, in his family for centuries, was indeed his home.

While still remaining true to the age-old architecture and the style so typical of the island, the interior had been modernized to make for very comfortable living. Several del Castillo families could, and had in the past, share the various apartments the castillo offered for private family living, if desired. Despite that, his brothers had chosen to make their own homes elsewhere on the island—Reynard in a luxurious city apartment overlooking the sparkling harbor of Isla Sagrado's main city, Puerto Seguro, and Benedict in a modern home clinging to the hillside overlooking the del Castillo vineyard and winery.

He understood why they each felt the need to carve out their own space but he still missed their presence around the castillo, for all the rare time he spent at home these days. Between himself and *Abuelo* there was a great deal of space to fill. A little more of the castillo had been filled today because Loren was inside right at that moment—waiting for him. Something about the thought of his bride-to-be newly settled in his home made it all abruptly real to Alex. After all the planning, she was finally here. In a few weeks, she would be his wife. And hopefully, in the not-too-distant future, the building would fill with the sounds of children again. *His* children. The thought made something deep inside him swell.

It would be good for *Abuelo* to be distracted from the rigors of growing old by the prospect of amusing the next generation of del Castillos. He had a wealth of family history to share. It was only right he have the opportunity to do so.

With that thought in the forefront of his mind, Alex swept his sleek black Lamborghini through the electronic gates and inside the walls, toward the stables that had been converted to a multicar garage thirty years ago. In minutes he was on the large curved stone staircase leading to the next floor, which housed the private suites of family rooms. Loren's was close to his own and he hesitated at her door, his hand poised to knock.

Something stayed his hand, and he let his fingers curl

instead around the intricately carved heavy brass handle of her door. It lifted smoothly, gaining him entrance. He would have to speak to her later about keeping her door locked. While the castillo's security was advanced, paparazzi were not above masquerading as one of the many staff, or even bribing them, in an attempt to get the latest scoop on the family.

Long silent strides on the thickly carpeted floor led him to her bedroom. There, sprawled across the covers, lay his future bride. Every nerve in his body surged to life as he observed her, arms and limbs askew, hair spread like a dark cloud around her head. There should be a childlike innocence about her, he thought, yet instead there was only the lure of her female form.

Small breasts pressed in perfect mounds against the fine cotton of the T-shirt she'd obviously chosen to sleep in. And only the T-shirt, he observed, keeping himself grimly in check even as he feasted on the sight of the faint outline of her nipples against the well-washed fabric. He tore his eyes from their gentle peaks and instead gazed upon the long slender length of her legs. Not one of his most sensible decisions, he thought as a heated pulse beat low in his groin.

One of her arms curved up and over her pillow, the other was flung out to one side, her unadorned hand curled like a delicate shell.

Alex dropped to his knees at her bedside and leaned over the mattress. He felt the warmth radiating from her, as if it were a tangible thing, as his lips hovered over the softness of her palm. Then he bent his head and pressed his lips against the fleshy mound at the base of her thumb, the tip of his tongue sweeping across its surface to taste her skin.

Loren's fingers curled to cup his cheek and he sensed

the precise moment she emerged from her slumber. Heard the sharp intake of breath through her lush pink lips. Saw the awareness flare in her eyes as her lids flashed open.

"Alex?"

Her voice was drugged with the residue of sleep yet its huskiness sent a lance of pure heat cutting through his body, provoking him to full, aching arousal. Right now he wanted nothing more than to sink onto the soft mattress with her, to envelop her in his arms and to taste all the delights her body had to offer. But he'd already promised to wait until their wedding night and they would be expected amongst company very soon. He forced his unwilling flesh to cooperate and gently pulled away from her touch.

"I know you're tired, but you must begin to ready yourself for dinner tonight."

"Dinner?"

She sounded confused. Surely Giselle had informed her of this evening's expectations.

"Yes, dinner. My grandfather looks forward to welcoming you back home."

He averted his gaze as she pushed herself upright and sat with her legs crossed beneath her. The creamy skin of her thighs and the shadowed hollow he knew lay at their apex, just beyond the hem of her shirt, were pure torment as he imagined touching her softness and delving into the hidden flesh there.

Arousal flared anew, this time even more demanding than before. But Loren's next words, delivered with an unmistakable note of challenge, doused his ardor as quickly as it had flamed into searing life.

"And you? Do you also welcome me home, Alex?"

Three

He fought back the flare of irritation that swelled inside him at her words. Was she criticizing him for not having been at the airport to welcome her? Giselle's insinuation echoed in the back of his mind. He fought for an edge of control, reminding himself she was no doubt still overtired from her journey and perhaps still wearing her disappointment he wasn't there to welcome her in person.

"Ah, I see you are still upset I was not at the airport to greet you. I thought Giselle explained why I could not be there."

"Oh yes, she explained." Loren unfolded her legs, threw them over the edge of the bed and rose to her full height.

Barefoot, the top of her head barely even reached his shoulder, and dressed as she was she gave an almost childlike impression. But there was nothing childlike in her demeanor, nor in the very female brand of dissatisfaction reflected in her eyes. He was reminded of the times he'd upset his mother. Never one to raise her voice, she'd only needed a look such as this to put him in his place.

"I would have been there if I could." Alex softened his tone. He should have made more effort to be at the arrival hall. He realized that now. He'd tried to make things easier for both of them, but instead he'd made matters worse. Still, the situation wasn't beyond salvaging and now he was determined to recover as much ground as possible.

"I have been looking forward to seeing you this evening," he said, his voice low.

He saw pleasure light her eyes and felt an inner relief as her full lips curved into a smile.

"So have I," she said shyly, dropping her gaze.

"So, you will dress for dinner and come down to share our repast?"

"Of course I will. I'm sorry I was a bit cranky. I'm never at my best when I first wake."

Alex allowed his mouth to relax into a smile. "I'll make a special note to remember that for after we're married."

She laughed, a delicious liquid sound that penetrated the last remnants of his temper and scattered them to the corners of the room.

"It might pay to." She smiled. "Now, tonight. What time and where? I'm assuming your family still dresses for dinner?"

She must have been half-asleep already when Giselle told her, he decided.

"Yes, we change for dinner. We meet for drinks in

the salon usually about eight and dine at nine. Late, I know, if you aren't used to it anymore."

"Oh, don't worry, I'll acclimate. Will you take me down?"

"You no longer remember where the salon is?" He cocked a brow at her.

"Of course, I don't imagine the castillo has changed all that much. I just…" She worried her lower lip with perfect white teeth. "No, don't worry. I'll meet you there at eight."

Alex dropped a chaste kiss on Loren's upturned face and moved away before the disappointment he sensed in her encouraged him to take more. Now that she was here and they were on the verge of achieving his goal of settling the governess's curse, there was no need to rush into anything. There would be plenty of time to kiss her the way he wanted—after they were married.

"Good girl. I'll see you there."

Loren watched her door close behind Alex's back and she fought the urge to stomp her foot in frustration. Now she was here he'd reverted to treating her like a child. Gone was the attentive lover who'd wooed her back in New Zealand. In his place was the old Alex she remembered so well. Slightly indulgent and full of the importance of his role as eldest son.

Well, she'd show him she was no infant to be coddled. Her body still hummed with her reaction to the soft kiss he'd pressed in her palm to wake her. Just one small caress and she'd shot to full wakefulness, her joy in seeing him only to be dashed by his reminder of her duty to be at some formal dinner tonight.

She knew they still adhered to the old ways, ways she'd taken for granted until moving to New Zealand with its more casual approach to lifestyle and mealtimes, but she'd hoped for a private dinner with her new fiancé. It wasn't so much to have expected, was it? Surely Alex's grandfather would have granted them this first night alone together?

There was nothing for it now, though, she reminded herself as the chime from an antique ormolu clock in her sitting room chimed the half hour. She had to fulfill Alex's expectations. At least she knew she'd have fun catching up with his brothers. As for Alex, well, maybe she'd punish him a little for not pressing to have kept her to himself tonight. She had just the perfect outfit in there. She'd bought it with Alex's reaction to her very firmly in mind.

She looked about her room for her suitcases and was surprised to see them gone. A quick look in her dressing room solved her problem as she espied her clothing already unpacked and hung neatly on hangers or folded away in the built-in drawers. She must have been totally out of it not to have heard the maid come in and see to her things.

She quickly filtered through the selection of dresses she'd bought, her hand settling on the rich red silk organza cocktail dress she wanted to wear tonight. The bodice was scattered with tiny faceted beads that caught the light and emphasized her small bust, while the layers of fabric that fell from the empire line below her breasts had a floating effect that made her feel as though she was the most elegant creature on the planet. Not a feeling she embraced often, Loren admitted silently.

She laid the dress on her bed and chose a pair of stiletto-heeled sandals in silver to wear with it.

"And if that's not dressed up enough for dinner, then nothing will do," she said out loud.

She made her way into her bathroom and took a moment to appreciate the elegant fixtures. The deep claw-foot bath beckoned to her but she knew she had little time left to get ready. She wondered briefly why Alex had acted as if she should have known all along about the dinner tonight. Perhaps Giselle had meant to tell her and had forgotten. Although Loren suspected that Giselle forgot very little indeed.

No, it must have been an oversight somewhere along the line. What with all the paparazzi at the airport, it was something that could easily have slipped Giselle's mind. She was prepared to be charitable. After all, she was finally *home*. Back on Isla Sagrado. Back with Alex.

She hummed happily to herself as she took a brief and refreshing shower. After toweling herself dry with a deliciously soft, fluffy bath sheet that virtually encased her from head to foot, she swept up her hair into a casual chignon and applied her makeup with a light hand. She studied her appearance for a moment then decided to emphasize her eyes a little more and to apply a slick of ruby-red gloss to match her dress. With the strength of color of her dress she'd disappear if she didn't vamp things up a bit, even if she normally only wore the bare minimum of cosmetics. Finally satisfied with her smoky eyes and glossy lips, she reached for a clean pair of panties and then slipped into her gown.

Loren loved the shimmer of the fabric as it brushed over her skin. The tiny shoestring straps and the low back of the dress made it impossible to wear a bra, but the beading hid any evidence that she was braless. She slid her feet into the high-heeled sandals and bent to do up the ankle straps before checking herself in the antique cheval mirror in her room.

Yes, she'd do nicely for her first meal at home with the del Castillo men, and for whoever else might be joining them. She wondered whether either Reynard or Benedict would have companions for the evening. Both of Alex's brothers' eligible bachelor status led them to be featured highly in magazines even as far away as New Zealand, and she doubted either of them would have far to look to find company.

A quick look at the clock on the bedroom mantelpiece projected her through her suite and out the main door into the corridor to the main stairs. She was grateful for the ornate carpet runner because she had no doubt her heels would have caught on the ancient flagstones beneath it as she hurried down the stairs.

For a moment the sense of longevity about the castillo seeped through her. How many del Castillo brides had traversed this very path to their betrothed over the centuries, and how many of those marriages had been as happy as she hoped hers and Alex's would be? She shook her head a little, chiding herself for being fanciful as a sudden weight of expectation settled upon her shoulders. A small chilled shudder ran down her spine, as if she was being watched—judged, even.

Loren hesitated on the stairs and looked around her, but of course there was nothing there but the gallery of portraits of successive heads of the family over the past many years. She injected a little more urgency in her step as she reached the bottom of the staircase and headed to where she remembered the salon to be.

The murmur of deep male voices, punctuated by the sound of laughter, was comforting as she approached the room where Alex had said to meet. Loren quashed the lingering effects of the sense of disquiet that had hit her earlier and focused instead on the prospect of an evening with the man she'd loved for as long as she could remember. Nothing could go wrong now, nothing. Her life was finally what she'd always dreamed it would be.

With a smile on her face, she entered the salon and was treated to the impeccable manners of four gentlemen rising from their seats to welcome her. Loren nodded in greeting to Reynard and Benedict, each easily recognizable and, she noted with some surprise, unaccompanied by female adornments.

Alex stood a little to one side. His hair, still wet from a recent shower, was slicked back off his forehead, giving him a sartorial edge that went well with the black suit and shirt he'd donned for the evening. But the serious set to his mouth and his darkened jawline made him appear unapproachable.

His dark eyes caught hers and burned beneath slightly drawn brows. She felt her smile waver a little under his gaze, but then he smiled in return and it was as if another giant weight had been lifted from her.

"You look beautiful," he said, his eyes glowing in appreciation.

A flood of pleasure coursed through her at his words, warming her all the way to her toes.

"Come, say hello to *Abuelo*. He has been impatient to see you."

She crossed the room, straight toward the silver-haired figure nearest the fireplace. Despite the fact it was May, a fire roared in the cavernous depths, throwing heat into the room and adding a cheerful ambience that chased the last of the lingering shadows from Loren's mind.

From his proximity to the fire she deduced Alex's grandfather felt the chill far more than he used to, and she couldn't help noticing the slight droop to one side of his face and the way he leaned heavily on an ebony cane. It saddened her to see he'd aged so much since she'd left, but one look at the spark in his eyes showed her that *Abuelo* was still very much the patriarch and very much in control.

Her lips curved in genuine pleasure as she placed her hands in his gnarled ones and leaned in to kiss him on the cheeks.

"Bienvenido a casa, mi niña," he murmured in his gruff voice. "It is past time you were back."

"It is so good to be home, *Abuelo*," she replied, using the moniker he'd insisted she call him back when she was a child.

"Come, sit by me and tell me what foolishness has kept you from us for so long."

The old man settled back into his easy chair and gestured to the seat opposite.

"Now, *Abuelo*, you know that Loren's mother insisted she move to New Zealand with her," Alex said, coming to stand behind Loren's chair and resting one hand upon her shoulder. "Besides, you cannot monopolize her when she is here to see everyone."

Loren felt the heat from his palm against her bare skin and leaned into his touch, relishing the sizzling contact.

"I do not see any ring upon her finger, Alexander. You cannot monopolize her while she is yet a free woman."

"Ah, but that is where you are wrong, *Abuelo*," Alex teased in return. "Loren is most definitely mine."

A fierce pang of joy shot through her, catching her breath, at his words. If she'd had any doubts, they were now assuaged.

Loren felt Alex's hand slide down the length of her arm, to her left hand. Clasping it, he drew her upright to face him. Butterflies danced in her stomach as she saw the intensity in his dark eyes. Alex was a man who obviously thought deeply, not sharing those thoughts with many, but if the possessive fire she glimpsed burning bright in his gaze was any indicator, she had no doubt that he was about to stake his claim to her before his family.

Alex slipped his free hand into his jacket pocket and withdrew it again.

"This is a mere formality, as Loren has already consented to be my wife, but I want you, *mi familia,* to witness my pledge to marry her," Alex announced as he revealed the ring in his hand.

"That's if she hasn't taken one look at us and changed her mind," Reynard taunted his elder brother and was rewarded with a quelling glare.

"I h-haven't. I w-wouldn't," Loren stuttered slightly as she saw the exquisitely beautiful, smooth, oval ruby set in old gold.

"Then this is for you," Alex murmured, sliding the ring upon her engagement finger.

The gold felt warm against her skin and the ring fit as if it was made for her and her alone. She'd recognized it immediately when he'd drawn it from his pocket. The del Castillo betrothal ring, handed down from firstborn son to firstborn son, had been in the family for centuries. The last woman to wear it had been Alex's mother.

The gold filigree on each shoulder of the ring had been crafted into delicate heart shapes and the stone appeared to take on a new glow against her skin.

"It's beautiful, Alex. Thank you," she said, lifting her eyes to meet his. "I'm honored to accept this."

"No, Loren, you honor me by agreeing to become my wife."

"I've always loved you, Alex. It's no more than I've ever wanted."

The air between them stilled, solidified, almost becoming something corporeal before Benedict interrupted them with two glasses of champagne. He thrust one at each of them.

"This calls for a toast, yes?"

He passed another glass to their grandfather before raising one of his own.

"To Alex and Loren. May they have many happy years."

A look passed between the brothers, something unspoken that hovered in the air as they connected silently with one another, then as one lifted their glasses to drink. Whatever it was, it was soon gone as sibling rivalry and teasing took over the atmosphere, leading even *Abuelo* to laugh and admonish them gently, reminding them of the lady in their midst.

Now she really belonged, Loren thought as she smiled and sipped the vintage French champagne, letting the bubbles dance along her tongue much as happiness danced through her veins. And, as the subtle lighting in the room caught the ruby on her finger, she knew that no matter how distant Alex had been today, everything was now perfect in her world.

Four

"I see he's given you that old thing."

Loren forced her shoulders to relax and her instincts not to bristle at Giselle's throwaway remark. It was three days after her arrival at the castillo and the first time she'd been forced back into Giselle's company. Days that had been filled with dress fittings and learning her responsibilities toward the staff at the castle. At least in the matter of her wedding dress she'd been able to choose for herself. As far as the wedding ceremony and reception went, Loren had been forced, with so little time left, to refrain from making any changes.

She chewed over Giselle's comment about the ruby. Clearly the woman wanted to belittle both her and Alex's gift, but she'd chosen the wrong target. What would the other woman know, or even begin to understand, of del Castillo tradition and the importance and validation behind having received the ring Alex had given her?

"I'd have asked for something more modern myself," the other woman continued.

Giselle lifted one hand from the steering wheel of the car in which she'd just picked Loren up from the castillo. Shafts of sunlight caught on the diamond tennis bracelet she wore on one wrist.

"Something more like this."

Loren merely smiled. "Your bracelet is beautiful, but I prefer knowing that there is only one of this ring and understanding the history behind it. I feel privileged to be chosen to wear it."

And she did feel privileged. Being given the family heirloom had cemented her place at Alex's side, no matter how emotionally and even physically distant he had remained since that night. She was confident that in time their emotional distance would close and eventually disappear altogether, especially if their reaction to one another was anything to go by. She closed her eyes and momentarily relived the pressure of his mouth against hers as he'd said good-night at the door to her suite on the night he'd given her the ruby. She'd all but ignited under his masterful lips and tongue.

She'd wanted to clutch at the fabric of his shirt and pull him toward her, to feel the length of his body imprint against hers as it had when he'd kissed her back in New Zealand. But he'd stepped away slightly—only allowing their lips to fuse, their tongues to duel ever so briefly, before pulling away and wishing her a good night's rest.

What would he have done, she wondered, if she'd taken him by the hand and pulled him into her suite and closed the door firmly behind them? Would he have taken her to her bed and finally taught her the physical delights of love that she'd only read about?

Her timidity frustrated her. What kind of woman was she, coming to marriage to a man of the world such as Alex with no experience beyond a few unsatisfying furtive fumblings and clumsy kisses? She was eager to learn from Alex, but anxious at the thought of disappointing him.

She cast a sideways glance at Giselle. No doubt she'd never faced such a conundrum. The woman looked as if she'd been born ready to take on the world and all its challenges. She also didn't look like the kind of woman to whom Loren could confide her insecurities.

She wondered who'd given Giselle the bracelet she wore so proudly. No doubt some man who'd found her particular brand of confidence and self-assurance as sexy as her lush figure and thick, cascading blond hair. She probably had an array of jewelry like it.

As if suddenly aware of her scrutiny, Giselle flicked her a glance.

"Where would you like to start today? Alex said you're to spare no expense on your trousseau. I imagine you were limited for choices where you lived in New Zealand."

"A little, yes, but aside from the usual imported labels we have access to our own wonderful designers, too. I just rarely had the necessity to dress up all that much."

Loren shifted in her seat, a little uncomfortable with the unspoken suggestion that her wardrobe lacked for anything. Had Alex said as much to Giselle? Did he even trust her to choose her own clothing? The answer was obviously no. Why else would he have insisted Giselle come with her today, when she'd already hinted she'd prefer to spend her time with him, not his assistant?

Besides, everything she owned was of excellent

quality, even if the outfit she'd chosen today lacked the European flair of Giselle's tailored trousers and open-necked silk blouse.

"Well, that will all change as Alex's wife, you know. You'll need a good range of items that can take you through any occasion. We frequently entertain royalty and overseas celebrities at the resort and Alex likes us to keep a personal touch with those special guests."

Giselle's casually possessive use of the words *we* and *us* struck Loren as more than accidental. Was she hinting that she had acted at Alex's side in a role as something more than merely his employee? They'd certainly have made a striking couple—he with his dark good looks and she with her golden beauty. Loren silently chastised herself for the pang of envy she felt. Giselle was Alex's right-hand person—of course she'd have escorted him on company business.

She took a steadying breath before replying, "Yes, we pride ourselves on that level of care at the station, too. You'd be surprised at the caliber of guests we have entertained there. But that was nothing new to me. As you know, I grew up here and my father was also a prominent member of Sagradan society. I'm well used to moving among royalty and celebrity and I look forward to accompanying Alex in the same regard. Now, with the shops, I think we should start from the skin out, don't you? I love lingerie shopping."

"Good choice. I know just the right shop to start at and Alex already has an account there."

Loren stiffened. There was no avoiding it. Alex kept an account at a lingerie store, which meant he was well accustomed to purchasing women's lace and finery—from the skin out. Taking a deep breath, Loren reminded herself that there could be an innocent reason for why he kept such an account—perhaps for those special guests that Giselle had already alluded to. Luggage went missing, or was delayed, every day around the world, and things were occasionally lost or damaged in hotel laundries. It would make perfect sense for him to hold an account, Loren rationalized silently.

But in spite of the logic of that explanation, a bitter taste settled in her mouth. Yes, Alex probably used the account for business reasons—but she was a fool if she thought that was the extent of it. Of course he was a man of the world and had no doubt had multiple lovers. Even as a teenager, she'd noticed the way women flocked to him. At the time, she'd dealt with it by trying to scare them all off, but she hadn't been naive enough to believe that she'd succeeded. And now she had proof. She didn't have to like it but she was going to have to learn to live with it, one way or another.

Unconsciously she twisted the heavy ruby ring on her finger. She hadn't expected any words of love from him when he'd given it to her, even though she'd expressed them herself. How could he have learned to love the person she was now, anyway? She'd changed so much from the sometimes petulant and demanding child he remembered. But they had plenty of time for him to learn to love her. They were to be married and she was going to do everything in her power to make it a long and loving marriage.

At the lingerie store Loren was overwhelmed by the multiple arrays of delicate fabrics and colors on offer. She fingered a satin-and-lace nightgown of the sheerest oyster pink. There was a matching wrap that had an exquisitely detailed lace panel in the back. She knew she had to have it.

"Oh, that's pretty," Giselle commented over her

shoulder. "But I wouldn't waste too much money on things like that. Alex isn't keen on night wear."

Loren stiffened again. And she'd know that snippet of information how? Okay, so maybe the other woman's earlier comments could have been misconstrued but there was no doubt that Giselle had ceased to be subtle about her allusions to things about which she appeared to have a very personal knowledge.

A needle of pain worked deep into Loren's chest. So, Alex had indulged in an affair with his beautiful assistant. May indeed still be doing so, for all she knew. Did he plan for it to continue even after their marriage? Loren swallowed against the bile that rose, sudden and foully bitter, in her throat.

Giselle still hovered at her side, her green eyes narrowed slightly as if gauging the result of her comment on Loren. Loren knew she had to say something—anything to get through the next few minutes—but she also knew that she dare not show any sign of weakness. A woman like Giselle would capitalize on that weakness and run with it and there was no way Loren was about to let that happen.

"Hmm," she murmured calmly, nodding slowly. "Good to know. Thanks, but I think I'll get it anyway."

She was rewarded with a sharp look from her companion, puzzlement followed swiftly by acceptance, as if Giselle realized that she'd made her point but had failed to rattle Loren as she'd so obviously intended.

It was a hollow victory.

The rest of the day stretched ahead interminably for Loren. The mere thought of absorbing and defusing more comments from Giselle extinguished every last moment of pleasure she'd anticipated in the day.

Loren suggested they take a break with a coffee at one of the harborside cafés. Once they were settled at their table and had placed their orders she sat back and let the warmth of the late spring sunshine seep into her body. She took a deep, steadying breath. She knew what she had to do.

"Giselle, look, I appreciate that you've taken time out of your day to help me with my shopping but I think I'd like a little time to myself and see if I can't catch up with some old school friends instead. You head back to the resort, I'm sure you have plenty of work you'd rather be doing. I'll just get a cab back to the castillo later today."

"Alex specifically asked me to assist you today. I can't leave you just like that," Giselle protested.

"Come on, let's be honest here. You don't want to spend time with me any more than I do with you. You've made it clear that you and Alex have a history. I accept that. But it is now very firmly in the past."

So back off, the unsaid words hung in the air between them.

Loren's heart hammered in her chest. She wasn't used to confrontation of any kind—avoided it like the plague on most occasions, to be honest. But when shoved hard enough she always stood her ground and right now she'd drawn her demarcation line.

"So you're sending me back to be with him? A bit risky, don't you think?"

The smile on Giselle's face was predatory.

"Risky? Well, it was me he traveled half the world to visit and asked to marry, wasn't it?"

Giselle snorted inelegantly. "Nothing more than the fulfillment of his duty to allay an old man's concerns and create some strong publicity for the del Castillo business empire. You can ask Alex about that yourself if you don't believe me." She bent and collected her handbag and rose gracefully from her chair. "Well, I can see I'm no longer wanted here. Far be it from *me* to stay where I don't belong."

Loren sat and watched Giselle walk away, the clear insult about Loren's presence on Isla Sagrado, in Alex's life, echoing in her ears.

But Giselle was wrong, Loren had no doubt about that. If anything, *Giselle* was the intruder here, not Loren. Not when Loren had been born and raised here. Not when Alex had brought her back. Her hands curled into tight fists in her lap. She did belong here, Loren repeated silently in her mind. She did.

When Alex returned to the castillo that night Loren half expected him to mention something about Giselle returning to the office early, or even insist that she avail herself of the other woman's expertise. She'd prepared at least a dozen responses to him by the time she'd finally returned home herself, her arms laden with parcels after a full afternoon of shopping on her own. Her feet ached with the miles she'd walked but inside she'd reached a state she could finally call happy. No matter what Alex said to her about Giselle, she wouldn't let it bring her down.

The number of people who'd recognized her, the old friends she'd indeed bumped into who had been excited to see her—all had made her feel so thoroughly welcomed back.

As it transpired, she hadn't needed a single one of her arguments. Alex was distracted all through the evening meal, letting *Abuelo* direct most of the conversation and listening to her tell him of all she'd seen and done during the day.

After their meal, Alex walked her to her suite as he did every night. As she unlocked the door he put out a hand to cover hers.

"Would you mind if I come in with you this evening?" His voice was deep and the sound caressed her ears like a lover's touch.

"Not at all," she answered with a smile as she swung the heavy door open and stepped inside. "Please, come in."

Loren's heart fluttered in her chest. Had Alex decided not to wait for their wedding night? Nerves, plaited with a silken thread of longing, pulsed deep inside, slowly stoking a furnace of heat within her. Her skin grew sensitive. So sensitive, even the newly bought gown she'd worn to dinner felt too heavy against her.

She turned to him, aware that her cheeks were warm and no doubt bore a flush of color quite at odds with the elegance of her appearance tonight. Her eyes raked over him. Ah, she never tired of drinking in the sight of his masculine beauty. Of the breadth of his shoulders as they filled the designer suit he wore with such effortless grace and style. Of the press of his chest against the crisp white cotton of his shirt. Even the way his throat moved above the knot of his silver-and-black striped silk tie mesmerized her.

Her mind filled with the prospect of placing her lips to that very point where she could see the beat of his pulse—of pressing her lips into his skin, allowing her tongue to caress that spot and taste him, tasting so much more.

She clenched her thighs against the sudden thrum of energy that coiled there. But instead of lessening the sensation, it only intensified it, sending a small shock of pleasure through her and driving a tiny gasp past her lips.

She felt as though she was poised on the balls of her feet, ready to move into the shelter of his arms and feel once more the press of his body against hers. Her whole body was attuned to the man only a few short feet away from her.

"There is something I need to discuss with you," Alex said, the abruptly businesslike tone of his voice quelling her ardor as suddenly as if she'd been drenched by a rogue wave on the rocky bay beneath the castle.

Was he now going to take her to task for her dismissal of Giselle today? Loren felt the lingering remnants of desire slowly flicker and die. She swallowed and took a steadying breath.

"Well then, would you be more comfortable sitting down? Perhaps I can pour you a drink?"

"Yes, thank you. A cognac I think. And pour one for yourself, too."

Did he think she'd need it? Suddenly Loren wished he had simply stuck with their usual routine. Even a noncommittal kiss at the door was bound to have been better than being castigated for rejecting his assistant's company. Not that she was going to take any criticism of her choice today without putting up a decent protest of her own. But was she ready to face the truth if she asked him about his relationship with Giselle?

She crossed the sitting room of her suite to the heavily carved dark wooden sideboard against one wall. She took two crystal snifters from within and then lifted the cut-crystal stopper from one of the decanters on the edged silver tray that sat on the polished surface. Alex's warm hand closed over hers.

"Here, let me pour, hmm?"

A fine tremor ran through her as his touch sent a sizzle of electricity coursing up her arm.

She pulled away from him and forced her suddenly uncooperative legs to take her over to one of the two-seater couches. She lowered herself onto the richly upholstered fabric, yet couldn't bring herself to sit back and relax against the cushioned back, instead perching on the edge.

Alex crossed the room and handed her one of the glasses. Loren bent her nose to the rim, taking a deep breath of the aroma of the dark amber liquid before lifting it to her lips and allowing the alcohol to trickle over her tongue and down her throat. She never normally drank hard spirits, but she had the distinct feeling that tonight she was going to need it.

She swallowed, welcoming the burn the distilled liquor left in its path, and watched as Alex sat down opposite her. He unbuttoned his jacket and reached inside, drawing out a folded paper packet. He carefully placed the packet on the coffee table between them, then took a sip of his cognac.

The liquid left a slight sheen upon his lips, capturing her gaze with the inevitability of a moth to a flame. He pressed his lips together, dissipating the residue, allowing her to look away.

"Is that what you want to discuss?" Loren pressed as he made no effort to explain the papers he'd laid before them.

"Yes. It's a legal document I need you to read and sign before we are married. Someone can take you into the notary's office tomorrow for it to be witnessed."

"What kind of legal document?" Loren asked, not

even bothering to point out that she could quite capably make her own way into the city.

Alex's dark eyes bored into hers. "A prenuptial document."

"Well, that is only to be expected," Loren said matter-of-factly, even as she forced herself to quell the swell of disappointment that rose within her. Did he really find such a document necessary?

As far as she was concerned, this marriage was forever. She had no desire and no plans to ever leave Alex, nor, if such a heartbreaking event should occur, could she imagine she would ever make unreasonable financial demands against him.

"Perhaps it would be best if you read it first. If you have any questions I'm sure the notary will be able to answer them for you."

Alex put down his glass and rose from his seat. "I'd better get going. I have an early flight tomorrow."

"Flight?" Loren asked. "Where? May I come with you?"

"It is nothing but a business trip to Seville. You would be bored. Which reminds me, you will need to ask Reynard or Benedict to take you to the notary as Giselle will be accompanying me. Actually, best to call on Reynard. Benedict drives like a demented race-car driver at the best of times and I would hate for anything to happen to you before the wedding."

Loren fought back the bitter disappointment his words evoked in her. "I'll bear that in mind," she replied through stiff lips. "When will you be back?"

"In a couple of days, certainly no more than three."

Three days away with Giselle? Loren felt the news

deep in her gut, as if it was a physical blow. Perhaps her earlier fears of today were true after all.

"Good night, then." Alex walked the couple of steps that brought him to her side and bent to kiss the top of her head before leaving the room.

As she watched the heavy door of her suite close behind him she blinked against the prick of tears that had begun behind her eyes. She would not cry. She would not.

Loren reached across the table, lifted up the legal packet and slid out the folded document. Her eyes scanned the information. As unaccustomed as she was to legal jargon it all seemed to make sense until she reached a paragraph headed up with the words *legal issue*.

She read the paragraph, then read it again to be certain she understood the terminology. If she was correct, to ensure the continuation of the del Castillo bloodline she and Alex must make love at the time when her body was at its most fertile, and to ensure the correct timing, her menstrual cycle was to be monitored. Even the details of the clinic she would be monitored by were in the agreement.

Loren let the papers slide from suddenly nerveless fingers.

The legalese twirled around in her mind, sentences fragmenting before joining back together. Did this mean that she and Alex would *only* make love when she was ovulating? That was, what? A span of a few days at most in each month. And what if she got pregnant? Would he still share her bed, still make love with her as a husband did with his wife? Or would her job have been done, leaving him free to go back into Giselle's arms?

Just what kind of marriage was she entering?

Five

Loren heard the knock at the door to her suite and wondered if perhaps her maid had forgotten something. She'd only just sent her away, preferring to spend these last few moments before her wedding alone. She picked up her voluminous skirts and went to open the door.

"Giselle!" Loren stepped back, startled to see the blonde there. She let her skirts settle back down to the carpet beneath her, the ivory French taffeta giving a distinctive rustle.

"My, don't you look every inch the fairy-tale princess," Giselle remarked, coming into the sitting room.

Loren tolerated the woman's scrutiny of the dress that was the fulfillment of all her childhood dreams. Yes, she did feel like a fairy-tale princess in the strapless gown. Somehow the words from Giselle's glossy red lips made the idea more of an insult than a compliment.

"Was there something you wanted?" Loren asked coolly.

"No, Alex asked me to come up and check on you. He thought you might benefit from some female company since your mother isn't here."

Loren bit back the retort that immediately sprang to her lips. She would not fight, not with anyone, on her wedding day.

"That's lovely of him. But as you can see, I'm fine, thank you."

She waited for Giselle to leave but instead she settled herself on one of the couches. Loren had to admit, she looked beautiful. The woman certainly knew how to make the most of her features. The dress she wore would have looked vampish on anyone else, but on Giselle it was elegantly sensual.

"You know, I have to hand it to you. I thought you'd have given up by now," Giselle said.

"Given up?"

"Well, how many women would have signed that prenuptial agreement, for a start? I know I certainly wouldn't."

"Perhaps you would if you loved your fiancé enough," Loren commented quietly. "As I do."

Giselle waved her hand as if dismissing Loren's words, the very gesture making Loren's spine stiffen in irritation. She'd wanted this time alone to reflect on her coming marriage, and particularly on the terms of the prenuptial agreement that Giselle had mentioned. Clearly, the blonde knew all about it, and that fact rankled with Loren. It should have been a private matter. One between her and Alex alone.

This past week had been such a whirl of activity with a museum opening to attend along with several charity functions, all of which gave her a taste for what her duties would be like as a del Castillo bride. She and Alex, while together for much of their waking moments, had barely had a moment alone to talk. Whenever she'd tried to bring the subject of the prenuptial document up, Alex had brushed it off until later. Now, today, was about as late as it could get and Loren was still unsure of where she stood on the agreement she'd eventually signed.

"Well, whatever," Giselle continued, oblivious to Loren's obvious displeasure in her company. "You've really gone above and beyond the call of duty. It's either incredibly naive of you to stick with it or incredibly kind."

"Kind?"

"To agree to the terms just to help the company out and keep an old man happy."

"I don't know what you mean. I'm marrying Alex because I love him. Because I've always loved him," Loren stated as firmly as she was able.

"Surely you're aware that Alex is only marrying you because of the curse."

"The curse?" Surely she didn't mean the old governess's curse?

Loren knew well the story of the woman who'd been brought to Isla Sagrado from the south of France to educate the daughters of one of the original del Castillos on the island—a nobleman from Spain. The poor woman had fallen in love with her employer and entered into an affair that had lasted years.

Legend had it that she'd borne him three sons, but that in view of the fact his wife had only borne him daughters, he'd taken her boys from her and he'd raised them as his legitimate issue, paying her off with a ruby necklace from the del Castillo jewel collection. Paintings in the family gallery that predated the nobleman showed the necklace, known as *La Verdad del Corazon*—the Heart's Truth. It was a stunning piece of chased gold with a massive heart-shaped ruby at its center. Loren had always privately believed that it was more the type of gift a man gave to his one true love than as payment for services rendered.

When the nobleman's wife died, however, he'd married another woman—one from a high-ranking family. In her misery the governess was said to have interrupted the wedding, begging her beloved to take her back. When her lover—and her sons—turned their backs on her, she cursed the del Castillo family. If, in the next nine generations, the del Castillos did not learn to live by their family motto of honor, truth and love, the ninth generation would be the last. With that pronouncement, she cast both herself and the Heart's Truth from the cliffs behind the castle and into the savage ocean. Her body was later found, but the Heart's Truth had been lost ever since.

Loren had always found the story to be truly tragic and, as a child, had often imagined a happier ending for the governess and her lover.

If the curse was to be believed—not to mention previous generations' total disregard for its power—it was responsible for the steady diminishment of the family over the past nine generations. But to believe that Alex was marrying her in an attempt to break the curse, well, that was just ridiculous. What happened three hundred years ago had no bearing on life today.

"Surely you must know of it. You're from here, after all, and the papers have been full of it, especially since the announcement of your engagement. The boys are the ninth generation—the last of the line. Old Aston was starting to have concerns that they would stay that way. Alex is trying to downplay it but you know what his grandfather is like once he gets an idea into his head. He believes he's even seen the governess's ghost. Can you imagine it? Of course, Alex would move mountains to please the old man—especially if it also happened to be good for business.

"Anyway, they came up with this fabulous publicity drive where they'd all get married and have babies to prove to everyone, their grandfather especially, that the curse isn't real."

Giselle laughed but Loren was hard-pressed to quell the shiver that ran down her spine. Even more so when she weighed the truth in the other woman's words. If, as she'd said, *Abuelo* was genuinely concerned about the curse, Alex *would* do anything to alleviate those concerns. It was the kind of man he was and his loyalty and love for his family were unquestionable.

Would that loyalty and love extend to her, she wondered, or was Giselle right and was Loren merely the means to an end?

Giselle rose from her seat and brushed an imaginary fleck of dust from her dress.

"Well, I can see you don't need me. I'll go down to Alex and let him know you're ready. The cars are waiting to take everyone to the cathedral."

"Thank you."

Loren forced the words past her lips and tried not to think too hard about the ceremony ahead.

She would much rather have married in the intimate private chapel that formed a part of the castillo's family history, but her wedding to Alex was to be quite a show. Visiting dignitaries from all over Europe would be in attendance along with the cream of Sagradan society. Hundreds of guests, if the lists she'd seen were any indication.

Hundreds of strangers.

As the door closed behind Giselle's retreating figure it struck Loren how alone she truly was. The few old school friends she'd managed to touch base with since her return all viewed her differently now. Sure, they were friendly, but it was as if there was an invisible wall between them. As if she was unreachable. Untouchable.

Well, untouchable certainly fit in well with how Alex had continued to treat her. Maybe he was saving himself, making sure he was locked and loaded for when they met the terms of their prenuptial agreement, she thought cynically. Or maybe he managed to sate his appetites elsewhere, a snide voice niggled from the back of her mind. She pushed the thought from her head but couldn't quite get rid of the bitter aftertaste in her mouth at the thought.

Loren crossed the sitting room to the large window that looked out past the castle's walls and over the landscape. The sun was hot and bright today, a portent of the burgeoning summer months ahead. The sky was a sharp clear blue, broken by slender drifts of cirrus cloud here and there. It was a perfect day to be married by any standard, so why then did she suddenly feel as if it was anything but?

Alex fidgeted with his cuff links for what felt like the umpteenth time today as he stood at the altar of the cathedral.

"Do that again and they'll fall off," Benedict cautioned from his side.

"Funny guy," Alex responded, but forced himself to relax.

He looked back across the rows and rows of guests, some faces he knew well, others hardly at all. The cathedral was packed. Today's ceremony would be the beginning of the new age of del Castillos that would lay old ghosts to rest, and everyone who was anyone wanted to be there to see it. He met *Abuelo's* stare from the front pew, the one carved with the del Castillo crest. The old man gave him a slow nod of approval and Alex felt his chest swell with pride. Any doubts he might have had about whether he was doing the right thing were nothing in the face of his grandfather's happiness.

"Do you know what the delay is?" Reynard asked. "Maybe she's got cold feet and has made a run for the airport."

Alex gave his brother a glare, but he felt a short sharp pang of concern. Loren had been different since he'd given her the prenup to read and sign. A little more distant and a little less eager to please. Had the agreement bothered her that much? Surely she could see the necessity for such an agreement without it affecting their marriage. The financial considerations of providing for her, should he die unexpectedly or should their marriage fail, aside, of primary importance was ensuring the next generation. Once that was out of the way then, well, they could take whatever came next at their leisure—a prospect that, he had to admit, filled him with pleasure. It had been hell keeping his hands off Loren these past two weeks, especially when she'd obviously been eager to take their relationship to an intimate level.

But tonight his wait would be rewarded. Granted, the timing of their union meant that their liaison tonight would not be part of the agreement they'd both signed. It would instead be the consummation of the promises they would make to one another before all these witnesses today.

The importance of those promises settled in his chest like a solid lump of lead, pressing down on his heart, his very honor. It didn't settle well with him to be pledging to love another for the rest of their days when, in truth, he didn't love her.

Love. It wasn't something he and Loren had discussed. Hell, it wasn't even something Alex had considered until she'd declared her feelings for him the night he'd given her the engagement ring.

When she'd first agreed to marry him back in New Zealand, he had assumed she cared for him, perhaps admired him a little the way she had when she was a child. He'd also *known* she was attracted to him—just as he was attracted to her. And she'd wanted to honor her father's memory, in much the same way that he'd wanted to ease his grandfather's mind. So Alex had been comfortable with the arrangement—with the idea of a marriage based on mutual regard, a healthy dose of desire and shared respect for family. Love had never been part of the plan.

But something about her sweetly serious declaration when she accepted his ring and gave him her heart had moved him unexpectedly, making him feel almost shamed. Was it fair to her to accept her love when he was not yet prepared to return it? A picture of his parents flashed through his memory. He wondered what they'd think of the choice he was making today.

They had known real love. It had been considered only fitting that if their light had to be extinguished so early that they die together. The avalanche that had taken them, while on a romantic skiing holiday together without their sons, had wiped out joy as the boys had known it up until that time. Yet they'd been lucky to have had *Abuelo,* who'd put his own grief aside to continue to guide and raise the three teenage boys whose anger at their parents' fate sought many outlets.

It had been *Abuelo's* steady love and firm hand that had brought them through. Love they reciprocated. Taking another look at his grandfather's beaming face, Alex knew that while he would not be telling the truth as he made his vows to Loren today, the gift of hope it would give his grandfather was worth far too much for him to give in to second thoughts now.

"Last chance to back out," Benedict said under his breath. Before Alex could respond, a sudden hush spread through the cathedral. The centuries-old organ, which had been delivering a steady medley of music, halted. The lump of lead in Alex's chest shifted, forming a fist around his lungs as all eyes turned to the main doors. They swung slowly open and a burst of sunlight filled the doorway, bathing the vestibule with its golden glow. And then, within the glow of light, a lone figure appeared.

The fist squeezed tighter as Alex realized how difficult this must be for Loren. In the face of her mother's blank refusal to attend their nuptials, he should have insisted she be accompanied on her journey down the center aisle of the cathedral—past the many assessing eyes of the glitterati and politically powerful. But she'd refused all offers from his brothers and *Abuelo.*

"My father will be with me in spirit," she'd said, holding that determined, fine-boned chin of hers firmly in the air, daring him to challenge her wishes. "I need no one else."

He'd had to accede to her wish. After all, it was the only thing on which she had insisted in all the matters pertaining to the ceremony.

The powerful organ began again and as Loren began to glide down the aisle toward him, Alex realized he'd misjudged his bride's strength and fortitude.

Pride suffused every cell in his body as she walked toward him with effortless grace—her bare shoulders squared and her spine straight, her slender neck holding her head high. Loren's skin gleamed against the strapless ivory gown that hugged her torso and exposed the gentle swell of her breasts before spreading into a bloom of fabric around and behind her. For the first time in his memory, Alex was speechless. Beneath the gossamer-fine veil that covered her head and shoulders and drifted down to her waist he caught glimpses of light striking the diamond tiara that had once been his mother's. The matching necklace, its design the inverted image of the tiara, settled against her luminous skin at the base of her throat and spilled in a gentle V over her collarbone.

Her face was composed behind her veil, her eyes avoiding contact with his, focused instead on the altar behind him. As she drew closer he could hear the swish of the fabric of her gown as it swept across the floor, could see the fine tremors that shook the opulent bouquet of early summer blooms she carried.

"Looks like lanky little Loren Dubois has really grown up, hmm?"

Reynard's voice in his ear snapped Alex from his trance.

"For once in your life could you just shut up?" he hissed at his brother through teeth clenched so tight his jaw ached, earning a glare of disapproval from the priest in the process.

Reynard's next words, however, shocked him in a way he never expected.

"Don't hurt her, Alex. Whatever you do, don't *ever* hurt her."

"Noted," Alex replied with a swift nod.

He met his brother's eyes briefly. There was no doubting Reynard meant what he said. For some strange reason it made him feel better that Loren had a champion. That it should have been him was not wasted on him at all, but given what he'd agreed to do to save the del Castillo family and fortunes, it was only fitting it be one of his brothers. Both, if the look on Benedict's face was any indicator.

A savage rush of possession roared through his veins. They could look, certainly, they could warn him as much as they liked, but essentially, Loren was his. As she joined him on the steps in front of the altar that knowledge gave him the ultimate satisfaction.

When it came time to say their vows, Loren looked at him, truly looked at him, for the first time that day. And as she pledged to love him, he found he had to look away. Her words carried such surety, such conviction. She deserved more than empty promises in return. Her voice wobbled slightly on the last word of the formal ceremony they'd chosen. No, he corrected himself, the ceremony Giselle had chosen. Shame scored him. This was Loren's wedding day. He should have given her more say in how the day was to go.

He'd approached this all wrong. He already had her love and loyalty and he'd walked roughshod over both in the execution of *his* goals and *his* needs. Loren was more than a means to an end, she was a vital, living, breathing woman.

He would make it up to her, he promised himself

silently. As soon as they'd fulfilled the first part of the prenuptial agreement, he would definitely make it up to her.

Loren had barely spoken half a dozen words directly to him since they'd exchanged their vows. In the car from the wedding reception it was no different. Alex found the uncharacteristic silence challenging. Normally Loren found something, anything, to talk to him about—it was one of the things he found so engaging about her.

But something had changed inside her today; he could sense it in the way she held herself, the way she'd spoken to others. As if she was playing a part and was not really totally involved in what she was doing.

As their car swung through the gate of the outer wall and drew up to the entrance of the castillo it finally occurred to Alex why she was so quiet. She had to be nervous about tonight. He would make sure their first time was one she would remember forever. A special night. A memory to be treasured.

Dios, but she looked exquisitely beautiful. He could almost taste the satin softness of her skin already. Almost feel the shiver of desire ripple across her skin.

As the driver opened his door he gave a short command to the man to allow Alex himself to escort his new wife from the vehicle. He walked around to her side of the car and pulled open her door, offering her his hand.

"Come, Loren. Let me help you inside."

"Thank you," she said softly.

The voluminous skirts and sweep of the train of her dress was a confection of fabric about her, yet she handled the garment with the grace of a swan. Another definite plus in her favor—no matter the situation, she handled it with aplomb. In spite of his concerns, he knew he'd chosen well when he'd decided to marry her. She would be a marvelous asset to him in so very many ways.

"You were wonderful today, I was so proud of you," he bent to murmur in her ear as they approached the arched entrance of their home.

"It was an—" she hesitated a moment before continuing "—interesting day."

"Interesting?" Alex forced himself to laugh softly. Surely she hadn't picked up on his unease during the ceremony—or had she? Well regardless, he'd have to put her mind at ease. "It was a great success. All of Isla Sagrado knows you are now my beautiful bride and their blessings upon us will reflect back upon them. I imagine, though, it must have been difficult for you."

"Difficult?"

"Without your family to support you."

"Yes, it was difficult, but it was what my father would have expected of me."

There was a note to her voice that sounded off-key but Alex pushed the thought aside. She was obviously weary after the pomp and ceremony of the day and the obligations she'd fulfilled at the lavish reception.

Alex guided Loren up the stairs and toward the shared suite he'd ordered their effects delivered to today—the suite that had been his parents'. As they swept inside he nodded in approval at the sensual soft lighting provided by the plethora of candles he'd requested be lit before their arrival.

The heady scents of rose and sandalwood drifted on the air, feminine and masculine, yin and yang.

"Would you like to be alone while you change? Or

perhaps I should call your maid to assist with your gown?"

"No, it's all right. I can manage the lacing myself," Loren replied.

Again there was that slight discordance. Again he shrugged it away.

"I'll leave you to change then."

She merely inclined her head and moved gracefully across the room to her private chamber. Alex watched as she drew the door closed behind her then wasted no time getting to his private en suite bathroom and divesting himself of his clothing before stepping under the hot steam of a quick shower. A few swift swipes of his towel later and he was dry. Naked, he padded through to his dressing room where he reached for midnight blue, satin pajama bottoms and a matching robe.

Would her touch be as soft as the fabric that caressed his skin, he wondered. No, it would be softer, he was certain. His body coiled tight in anticipation of what lay ahead.

Before he realized it, he was at the door to her rooms, his hand twisting the handle and thrusting open the door. Candles had been lit in here, too. The large pedestal bed, swathed in cream-and-gold draperies, stood invitingly empty.

Empty?

A sound drew his attention as his bride came from her bathroom. Her satin nightgown skimmed her slender form enticingly, cascading over her gentle curves much as his hands now itched to, also. A small frown puckered her brow as she worked a brush through her hair.

"Here, let me," Alex said as she crossed the room. He took the brush from her fingers. "Sit down on the bed."

Loren did as he requested and Alex stood a little behind her and forced himself to focus on her hair and only her hair as he reached to stroke the brush through her tresses, easing out the knots and occasional forgotten hairpin.

"Ah." She sighed. "That feels wonderful."

Liquid fire pooled in his groin at her words. He planned to make her feel so much more wonderful very soon. Now that the brush flowed more smoothly through her hair he allowed himself to focus on the deliciously smooth, bare shoulders she presented to him.

Palest pink straps of satin were all that held her nightgown up. Straps that with the slightest breath could slide down those shoulders and farther, down her slender arms, exposing her back. He'd never found the prospect of observing a woman's back so enticing before. But then again, with Loren everything was different. Everything felt new.

He couldn't help himself, he had to taste her. He gathered her hair in one fist and gently drew it away from the nape of her neck then bent to kiss her, allowing his tongue to stroke across her skin in a private caress.

He felt her response ripple down her spine. Smiling to himself, he kissed her again—this time sucking gently—and was rewarded with the soft sound of her gasp. Alex let the hairbrush drop to the floor and placed both his hands upon her shoulders, coaxing her upright to turn and face him.

Her face, clean of the makeup she'd worn today, appeared flushed in the candlelight—her eyes luminous, their pupils dilated so far they almost appeared to consume the dark velvet brown of her irises. Her lips were moist and remained slightly parted. His gaze dropped to her breasts, to the clearly delineated pinpoints of her nipples as they thrust against the satin with her each and every rapid breath.

Something knotted tight and low in Alex's belly. Something possessive. Something wild. Every instinct within him roared that he plunder her lips, that he drag the delicate fabric of her nightgown from her body and expose her to him, allowing him to feast on her feminine glory. To rush her to dizzying heights she had no experience of.

To mark her as his own.

She is inexperienced, he reminded himself sternly, forcing himself to hold back, to slow down.

He let his hands skim across her shoulders and gently cup the back of her neck, tilting her head to him. He lowered his face, his eyes locked upon hers. His entire body rigid with the need to take this as gently as humanly possible.

His lips were only millimeters from hers. Already he could feel her breath against him, smell the sweetness of her breath.

"Alex, wait!"

Through the cloud of passion that controlled him he heard the plea in her voice. He closed his eyes for a moment and drew in a shuddering breath, constraining his desire.

"You are frightened. I'm rushing you. Do not worry, Loren. I will make tonight one you will never forget."

"No, it's not that," she said, pulling out of his arms, creating a short distance between them.

Already his body cried out for her. Craving her slender frame against his, aching for her warmth to envelop him.

"Then what is it?" he asked, fighting back the edge

of frustration that threatened to spill over into his voice. He didn't want to frighten her more with his hunger.

"It's about us. Our marriage."

"Us?"

A cold finger of caution traced a chilly path down his spine. What was she speaking of? They were married. Tonight would see the consummation of that marriage.

"Yes, Alex, us. I love you. I've always loved you one way or another. I accept that you don't return my feelings in the same way."

"You know I care for you, Loren," he asserted, determined to salve her concerns as quickly as possible.

"I know you do, but more as a brother would a sister."

"Believe me, my feelings toward you are most definitely not brotherly."

"Be that as it may." She waved her hand to disregard his words. "Even knowing you don't love me, I agreed to marry you in part because of my feelings for you, but also to honor my father and his promise to yours." She lifted her eyes to him. Eyes that glistened in the candlelight with unshed tears. "Can you honestly tell me that you have done the same?"

Tell her he'd married her to fulfill their fathers' vow to one another? No, not even he could lie about that. Not after the lies he'd already told before his grandfather in the church today. Lies that still coated his tongue with a tang of unpleasantness. The old promise was the reason he'd chosen to seek her out rather than find a bride on Isla Sagrado, but it was not the sole reason he'd decided to marry.

"No," he responded, his voice flat and tinged now

with the anger he bore toward himself more than to her. "But you have asked me to be honest. If you do not like my truth then you have only yourself to blame."

"But you have married me with the intention of producing an heir, is that true?"

She stood upright before him, holding her chin high, her shoulders straight, demanding his response.

"Of course."

"To dispel the governess's curse?"

Words failed him momentarily.

"The curse is nothing but an overstated legend. It has no bearing on us or on our marriage."

"So you didn't suddenly decide to travel all the way to New Zealand and then to marry me to put *Abuelo's* mind to rest? To prove that the curse wasn't real? Can you truly say that if it hadn't been for the curse you would *ever* have followed through with our fathers' wishes?"

He couldn't answer, to answer truthfully would damn him forever in her eyes—to tell a lie was impossible on top of the abomination of falsehoods he'd committed already.

"I see," Loren continued. "Well, then. It appears that we are at an impasse. I could have accepted almost anything from you, Alex, but I will not accept deception. You brought me here under false pretenses."

"You say you love me, and you did sign the prenuptial agreement," Alex reminded her, the words like gravel on his tongue. "You cannot back out now."

"I will meet the expectations of that agreement. You will have your heir, Alexander del Castillo, but I see no reason why we should enter into a physical marriage." A sharp note of bitterness crept into her voice. "In this day and age of technology why would you even want to consider the hassle and inconvenience, or indeed even the inconsistency, of making *love?*

"After all, if the act is to be as clinical and bereft of mutual affection as I imagine it will be, surely a petri dish will do, as well."

Loren's words hung like icicles in the air between them. Anger welled and rolled within him, much like the violent surf they could hear from the beach below through her open casement windows.

"You are refusing me your bed?" he finally managed through a jaw clenched so tight he thought his teeth might shatter.

"No. I am refusing you my body."

Six

Loren barely dared draw breath.

Alex stood before her, magnificent in his anger. Were she less determined about her decision she would have quailed in the face of his fury. To be honest, were she less determined she would have given in to the rush of longing that had drawn through her body like a fine silken thread as he'd touched her.

All her life she'd waited for the day that Alex would turn to her and welcome her into his life, and into his arms. Too bad that when that day had finally come she'd been forced to spurn him. She had never believed it would matter so much to her that he had hidden from her his true reasons for entering into their marriage.

In the lead-up to the wedding it had been enough for her to believe, however misguidedly, that they stood a chance of making their marriage work. But in the stark face of what she'd learned today, it was clear that Alex hadn't been above using her to get what he wanted. That it was for his family didn't assuage the hurt deep inside her. Nor the anger she bore at herself for having been such a blind and love-struck fool where Alex was concerned.

That she loved Alex with a passion that went soul deep was undeniable. But now she realized it most definitely wasn't enough. In her naïveté she'd thought she could change his perception of her as a child to that of a woman. A woman capable of great passion and unswerving loyalty.

Clearly she was still that naive child to have thought she could make a difference—make him begin to love her. He'd taken advantage of the promise made between her father and his and, shamefully, she'd let him. She was no innocent in this. She should have known and understood what was at stake. She should have asked questions, demanded answers.

But, no. She'd been focused on fulfilling a childhood dream. Of returning to the land of her birth and of being his bride. She'd allowed herself to be duped—heck, allowed? She'd been a fully willing participant into a marriage that stood no chance of being real right from the beginning.

Well, now he had his bride. He had his baby-making machine. That didn't mean she needed to debase herself any further by pandering to his machinations. Whatever the scheme he'd hatched with his brothers, she would do no more than her duty. She would give him the baby he required, but she'd find a way to live through this with what was left of her dignity intact.

"I think you'd better leave," she said, her voice breaking on the last words as she struggled to hold back the tremors that threatened to turn her into a quivering wreck.

Alex's eyes narrowed as he continued to stare at her in silence.

"P-please, Alex. Go."

"This is not over, Loren. I am not a man who likes to be thwarted."

Loren didn't answer, instead turning her back even as her chest throbbed with the pain of rejecting him and her eyes burned with the tears she refused to shed in his presence. She had what was left of her pride and she would not let that go. Not for anything. Not for anyone. Not even the man she loved with every heart-wrenchingly pain-filled breath in her body.

Behind her, Loren heard her chamber door close with a gentle sound. The fact he hadn't slammed the door behind him spoke volumes to the measure of his control. Control he would no doubt have been exerting over her behind the filmy curtains of her pedestal bed right now, had she let him.

Something twisted deep inside her, something sharp and raw, and her inner muscles clenched on the emptiness. She looked at the bed now and knew she would not sleep there tonight. She could not.

Loren crossed to the deep-set casement window that had been flung open to the velvet night. Despite the warm night air that coursed past her to fill the room, Loren was suddenly beset by a chill that went to her very bones.

Without a doubt spurning Alex tonight was the hardest thing she'd ever had to do in her life—the hardest decision she'd ever had to make.

Her fingers gripped the age-old stone of the window

ledge so tight they became numb, and she stared out at the night sky wishing things could have been so very different.

The sound of gentle knocking at her bedroom door woke Loren from the fitful slumber she'd finally fallen into around dawn. She straightened from the chaise longue she'd eventually sought rest upon and quickly threw her pillows and the comforter back onto the bed. Everyone knew how servants gossiped and, despite their loyalty to the del Castillo family, the staff here were no different.

She crossed the room to unlock the door and took a rapid step back when she saw it was not her maid, but Alex standing on the other side.

"*Buenos días,* Loren. I trust you slept well?"

He was absolutely the last person she expected to see this morning. She'd anticipated being totally left to her own devices after her rejection of him last night. Instead, here he was, looking and smelling divine. As if what had transpired between them had never happened. As if she'd never rejected him.

"As charming as your nightgown is, you will need to change for our excursion today."

"Change?"

"Of course, unless you want to be seen out and about Isla Sagrado in your night wear."

"We…we're going out? I thought—"

"Yes, I'm sure you thought that after last night I would not want to be near you. You underestimate me, Loren. We are newly married. We are expected to be seen together. Do you honestly believe that after everything I've put in place to make our marriage happen that I would just dissolve into the castle walls because you have decided we are not to sleep together?"

There was a dangerous edge to his voice. A hint of a reined-in temper simmering just beneath the surface of his urbane exterior.

"Of course not. I don't know what I thought, to be honest." Loren dragged in a breath, her senses instantly on alert as his fragrance infiltrated her confused mind and sent her pulse hammering in her veins. "When do you want me to be ready?"

"Our first appointment is in about half an hour, near Puerto Seguro, so about five minutes ago would be ideal."

"Appointment?"

"Yes, a tradition in my family when someone marries."

Thinking it was to be with the family lawyer, Loren spun away and yanked open her wardrobe, choosing a slim-fitting ice-blue suit. Her arm was stayed by Alex's hand upon her. She couldn't help it, she flinched, and didn't miss the frown that descended over Alex's features. He pointedly withdrew his hand from her bare skin before speaking.

"That's too formal. Wear something comfortable but smart."

Without any further information he spun on his heel and left her room. For a moment she just watched him. Her eyes drinking in the beauty of his movement, the breadth of his shoulders beneath the lightweight cream shirt he wore teamed with dark caramel-colored trousers. The way those trousers skimmed the cheeks of his buttocks.

She forced herself to blink, to break the spell he'd unwittingly woven about her, enticing her. She shoved the suit back into the wardrobe and flicked through her hangers, finally settling upon a black sundress with an abstract white print patterned upon it, relieving the starkness of the background. A mid-heeled pair of strappy sandals would hopefully give the outfit just the right balance Alex had specified.

Gathering her dress and a fistful of clean underwear, Loren swept into her bathroom. She wanted nothing more than to wash her hair but she doubted time would allow it. She swept its length into a shower cap and stepped beneath the stinging spray of the shower before the water had even reached temperature, gasping slightly against the cold.

She reached for the shower gel and liberally lathered it over her body. Had things been different, she wondered, would it be Alex's hands sliding over her skin now? Her nipples beaded into tight buds at the thought. Shaking her head at herself, Loren quickly rinsed off and stepped out of the shower cubicle and reached for a towel to dry off.

It only took a moment to dress and spritz a light spray of perfume on her pulse points. Her hair she brushed into a fiercely controlled ponytail, which she then braided and pinned in a spiral against the back of her head, all the while trying to forget how it had felt last night as Alex had brushed her hair. He'd shown her a tenderness she knew he'd have brought to his lovemaking—had she let things get that far.

Her reflection, however, definitely gave her pause. The sleepless night had left dark shadows beneath her eyes. It would take everything she had in her cosmetic arsenal to restore some semblance of the dewy bride Isla Sagrado had seen yesterday.

It took her a further ten minutes but by the time

Loren met Alex in their communal sitting room she was satisfied that she could cope with anything the day brought.

"Where are we going?" she asked as she checked her handbag for her sunglasses.

"You'll see when we get there," Alex responded enigmatically.

"What about breakfast?"

"Breakfast was a couple of hours ago but there will be a morning tea where we are going. Can you wait until then?"

Loren hazarded a look at her husband from under her lashes as she pretended to search in her bag for something else. *Her husband!* The solid truth of those two words rammed into her chest and clutched at her heart with a sudden twist. At her sharply indrawn breath, Alex gave her a look.

"Is everything all right?" he asked.

"Fine, I'm fine," Loren hastened to assure him. "And yes, I can wait for something to eat."

"Then we should be on our way."

He held the door to their suite open and escorted her along the wide corridor and down the sweeping stairs to the front entrance of the castillo. There, in the massive entrance hall, the staff had all assembled in a line, some bearing small gifts, others with nothing to give but the warmth in their hearts and the smiles on their faces.

How could she have forgotten the age-old Sagradan custom? It was tradition that the staff celebrate the master's marriage with offerings. On that occasion, the master and mistress of the property would also give the staff a small monetary gift.

"Have you—" she started to ask in a whisper.

"I have it under control," Alex assured her as one

by one they greeted the people who worked tirelessly behind the scenes in the castillo.

As she went forward to accept each small gift— some traditional in the old ways, such as the symbol of fertility that was pressed into her hand by the cook, and some modern—Alex in turn gave each staff member an envelope.

By the time they reached his waiting Lamborghini outside, Loren's arms were full of the tokens bestowed upon them. She made it into the car without dropping a one, and once settled she allowed them to tumble gently into her lap. Alex reached behind her seat to extricate a box and passed it to her before turning the key in the ignition and easing the car into gear and out through the castle gates.

Loren gently placed each token into the box, her fingers lingering on the Sagradan symbol of fertility, an intricately carved egg, before placing it inside and closing the lid.

"That was lovely," she commented, her hands firmly holding the box on her lap as they drove along the coastal road toward Puerto Seguro.

"You think so?" Alex asked, raising one dark brow. "I wouldn't have thought you'd have cared."

"Of course I care. Why would you think I wouldn't?" Surprise brought a defensive tone to her voice.

Alex merely shrugged and Loren felt herself bristle at his nonchalance.

"Don't judge me by your other women," she said quietly, but with a strong hint of steel.

"Don't worry, I wouldn't dream of it," Alex replied. "You are nothing like them."

Unable to come up with a suitable response, Loren lapsed into silence. She watched the road ahead of them through burning eyes and wished things could have been different. Of course she was nothing like his other women. If the tabloids had carried even an ounce of truth, those women had been confident, sophisticated and unerringly beautiful. Women like Giselle, for example.

For what felt like the umpteenth time, Loren castigated herself for having hoped for anything else from Alex other than what she'd ended up with. She knew better than most that life was no bed of roses. The only child of parents who'd loved passionately and fought bitterly, she'd seen what a push-me-pull-you state marriage could be. And she'd experienced firsthand the pain that ensued when such a marriage irrevocably broke down.

But at least her parents had enjoyed many years together before the cracks had started to show. It was more than what her immediate future held, unless she was fortunate enough for a fertilization procedure to work on the first attempt. If she could fill her life with a child then she could quite possibly manage to be happy.

Loren was unfamiliar with the building they now approached. A cluster of paparazzi was waiting at the entrance. Of fairly recent style, it was a large sprawling construction set in lush gardens and toward the back she caught a glimpse of what looked like playing fields. Was this some kind of school? She wondered what del Castillo family tradition called for a bride and groom to visit a school the morning after their wedding.

She recognized the family coat of arms carved into the lintel above the door but aside from that one claim of ownership there was nothing about the building to tell her of its purpose. At least not until they set foot inside. Muffled giggles and shushing sounds came from behind closed doors.

Children? At school on a weekend?

Alex laced his fingers through hers and Loren closed her eyes briefly in an attempt to quell the sudden surge of electricity that flared across her skin at his touch. The double doors ahead of them opened and, as they walked into what appeared to be a small auditorium followed closely by the media contingent, the air filled with the sound of children's voices in song.

Loren couldn't hold back a smile as the pure notes swirled joyfully around them.

"Who are they?" she whispered to Alex.

"Orphans, for the most part. Some are from families who cannot afford to feed and clothe them. They are the lucky ones for at least they have someone."

As the song drew to a close, one little girl separated from the bunch. In her hands she clutched a colorful bouquet of flowers. The caregiver behind her gave an encouraging little push in Loren's direction, but as the child drew closer a barrage of camera flashes filled the air and she tripped and started to fall forward. Loren reached out and caught the little girl before she could face-plant on the hard wooden floor. Some of the flowers, however, did not fare as well and when the child saw their snapped-off heads her lower lip began to wobble.

"Are these for me?" Loren asked, setting the child on her feet and kneeling down in front of her, ignoring the rapid-fire clicks and whirs of the shutters of the cameras trained on them.

The girl nodded shyly, one tear spilling from her lower lid and tracking slowly down a chubby cheek.

"Thank you, they're beautiful." Loren bent forward

and kissed her on the forehead. "And look, here's a flower just for you."

Placing the bouquet gently on the floor beside her, Loren pinched off one of the damaged blooms and tucked it behind the little girl's ear, securing it there with one of the pins from her own hair.

With both disaster, and further tears, averted, the little girl happily scampered back to her group.

"Nicely done," Alex murmured in her ear as he helped Loren rise to her feet.

She hoped he didn't see how his praise affected her, and that he missed the fine tremor that shook the bouquet she now held in her hands as if it was her most precious possession.

The rest of the morning passed uneventfully as she and Alex shared tea with the children and sat through a delightful series of performances. They were then led on a tour of the orphanage and Loren felt her heart break as she was shown the nurseries and the babies there. Under Alex's silent gaze, she took the time to cuddle each one and spent several minutes discussing their welfare with the nurses charged with their care.

By the time they took their leave and got back into his car Loren was shattered. Her arms still ached to hold the parentless children, as if by doing so she could somehow alleviate the harsh blow life had dealt them.

"You did well," Alex commented as they pulled away.

"It was nothing. I adore children, I always have."

"Especially the very young ones."

"Yes, especially them. They've had little opportunity to know love and of anyone they probably deserve it the most." Loren sighed and gently stroked the petals on the now rather tired-looking bouquet she'd been given. "What happens to them?"

"The babies or all the children?"

"All of them."

"Those that can be, are fostered with families on the island. We try and keep extended family involved wherever possible. Sometimes that's not an option, however. Others, like the babies and the toddlers, are usually adopted within months of their arrival at the orphanage. For the ones who remain, they are provided with schooling and, given their aptitude, they have the opportunity to earn scholarships to train in their chosen fields. Of the nurses and teachers there, at least half are returning children."

Loren nodded. She could understand why. The atmosphere there had been one of a strong sense of community and home, as far as they could manage on such a scale.

"Does the orphanage have a patron?"

"Not officially, not since my mother died. It has always traditionally been a del Castillo bride who becomes the orphanage's patroness. Between *Abuelo* and myself we have done what we can but some things definitely require a woman's touch."

"I'd like to take that on."

"You don't have to."

"No, I know that. But I want to, if that's okay."

Loren turned to look at Alex and saw him nod slowly.

"Then it looks as if tradition will live on, hmm?"

"Yes," she said emphatically. "It will."

Loren noticed they were now driving away from the city but not toward the castillo.

"Are we expected somewhere else today?"

"Yes," Alex responded, his eyes on the road ahead.

"Well, are you going to tell me where?" Loren demanded, suddenly feeling decidedly snippy.

The emotional toll of the orphanage visit, on top of the demands of their wedding day only yesterday and the distress of last night were all making themselves felt. She wanted nothing more right now than some peace and quiet.

"Look, I'm not up to any more of your cloak-and-dagger stuff. If you won't say where we're going you may as well let me out of the car right now and I'll find my own way home."

Alex still didn't respond.

"Stop the car," Loren demanded.

"We're almost there."

"Almost where?"

Loren looked around her but all she could see were fields and trees. Then, just in the distance, she caught sight of a series of domed buildings and a fluorescent wind sock on a tall pole.

"An airfield?" she asked. "Why are we going to an airfield?"

"Because our plane leaves in a short while."

"Our plane?" Loren felt as if all she could do was dumbly question everything that came from Alex's mouth.

"Yes, our plane."

She clenched her fists in frustration. Getting information from him was like getting blood from a stone.

"And where would this plane be taking us?" she inquired acerbically, fighting the urge to shout.

"On our honeymoon, of course."

Seven

"Honeymoon?"

Loren's voice reached a pitch that should have made Alex's ears ring. He turned to his new wife and smiled.

"It is usual for a newly married couple, and it is expected of us."

"But my things?"

"Await you on the plane."

"But what about…"

As Loren's voice trailed off he allowed himself a moment of satisfaction. She may have won the first round but this one was definitely his. Until her refusal of his attentions he would have been happy to remain at home on Isla Sagrado with her for their honeymoon as he'd originally planned. But she'd laid down a gauntlet when she'd spurned him last night. He was unaccustomed to anyone saying no to him—least of all the woman who had become his wife. He had serious ground to recover if this marriage was to work.

Her words had plagued him until dawn this morning, when he'd realized what he would have to do. It would be too easy for Loren to avoid him if they stayed at the castillo, or even if they'd gone to avail themselves of one of the luxury holiday homes on the other side of the island. No, he had to take her away, get her wholly to himself.

During their trip to the orphanage it was a simple matter to have her maid pack her things and have them delivered to the private airfield. Her passport and other papers were already in his possession, having been necessary for the legal paperwork of their marriage. A short call to a friend who owned a private holiday villa in Dubrovnik, a mere two-hour flight away on the Croatian coast of the Adriatic Sea, and his plan was in action. Only five minutes out of Dubrovnik old town, the two-bedroom stone cottage was a fifteenth-century delight. Private, fully modernized and the perfect setting for the seduction of his wife.

"Loren, you have nothing to worry about. Trust me."

"Trust you?" She snorted inelegantly. "That's rich, coming from the man who lied to marry me. The man who played on my own sense of values to get what he wanted."

A burr of irritation settled under Alex's skin, aimed more at himself than at her. He couldn't deny that she was painfully right.

"And what did you want, *mi querida?*" he asked, not bothering to hold back the cynicism that laced his endearment. "Don't tell me that you, for your own part, didn't use me a little, also?"

"I never lied to you," she answered quietly, her eyes impossibly somber as they met his.

For a few seconds the air between them thickened with the pain of the emotions he saw reflected in her gaze, and for a brief moment he tasted the bitterness of shame on his tongue. But he could not afford to dwell on his wrongdoing. They were now married and that was final. How successful would their marriage be? Well, that would no doubt depend on the next two weeks.

According to Loren's doctor at the clinic, based on her normal cycle, she would be entering her most fertile time soon. If his plans remained on track there would be no need for the detached methods she'd insisted were the only way she'd get pregnant with his child.

"Come," Alex said, getting out the car and going around to the passenger side to open her door. "The pilot is waiting."

"Where are we going?"

Sensing she'd had enough of secrets, Alex didn't beat around the bush. "Dubrovnik. We can be alone there."

He felt her shrink away from him as the words sank in.

"I hope they have a good selection of reading material," she commented tartly.

Alex laughed out loud, the humor in it startling even himself. If he knew his friend, any reading material would be eclectic and with a heavy emphasis on both cooking and eroticism. Suddenly he couldn't wait to get there.

The flight in the chartered jet was smooth and over within two hours, and it took very little time to clear customs and immigration. The midafternoon sun was bright and hot as they made their way to the waiting car outside the terminal building. Through it all, Loren maintained an icy silence. A silence that Alex looked forward to thawing, one icicle at a time.

The water in the little bay, fifty yards below where the cottage perched on the hillside, was a clear crystal blue. So clear you could even see the rocks and pebbles on the seafloor. Steps had been hewn from the rocky face leading down to the private beach. The cottage itself was a delight. Despite its aged appearance from the outside, Alex had been reassured to discover the interior was comfortably appointed and supplied with everything they would need for the duration of their stay.

He'd asked that the refrigerator-freezer and pantries all be fully stocked, and had stipulated that the cleaners were only to come when he could ensure they were away from the property. He wanted no interruptions to this idyll.

Loren was outside now, on the rear terrace, gazing out at the calm seas, a light breeze tugging at the severe hairdo she'd worn since this morning. Alex's fingers itched to take her hair down and to see her relax. As tense as she was now it would take days for her to unwind. He left the narrow kitchen area and walked across the tiled open-plan living area to where she stood.

"How about a swim before we have an early dinner?" he asked, coming out onto the terrace.

"An early dinner and bed sounds good to me."

"What, not game to tackle the steps?" Alex teased, reaching out a hand to caress her bare shoulder.

She stepped out of reach and sighed. "No, Alex, I'm not game to tackle the steps. In fact I'm not game for anything right now but something to eat and a decent night's sleep."

He gave her a thorough look. She did indeed look washed-out, with the pale strain of tiredness about her eyes more visible now than earlier. He gave a small nod.

"Okay," he said softly. "It's been a busy couple of days. Why don't you shower and change into something comfortable and I'll prepare something for us to eat."

"What? You? Cook?"

Ah, so she was not so tired that she couldn't insult him. That at least was mildly promising.

"I cook very well, as you'll soon discover. Now, you'll find the bedrooms downstairs. If you don't like the one where your cases are, we can swap."

Her eyes widened. "We have separate rooms?"

"Of course. Separate rooms, separate bathrooms. Unless, of course, you'd rather share?"

"No! I mean, no, that's fine. I thought…"

Alex knew exactly what she thought, but he was prepared to bide his time.

"Go on. Freshen up. Take your time, hmm? I want to shower and change myself before starting our meal."

He watched as she walked back inside the cottage and made for the stairs that led to the two bedrooms on the lower level. Yes, he was prepared to bide his time—for now. But he would not wait forever for his recalcitrant bride to accept the very real attraction that lay between them, nor the pleasure he was certain they would find together when she did.

"Loren, wake up. Dinner is ready."

Alex's voice pierced the uneasy slumber Loren had fallen into after taking her shower. The wide expanse of bed, with its pale blue coverlet and fresh cotton pillow slips, had proven too much of an enticement. She stretched as she stirred, forcing her eyes open.

The sun was much lower in the sky now, its light sparkling across the water visible through the floor-length windows like a thousand diamonds skipping across the waves.

Loren pushed herself upright, then snatched at her robe as she felt it slide away from her, exposing her nakedness beneath.

"If you'll give me five minutes, I'll be with you," she said as coolly as she could, hyperconscious of the hot flare of interest in Alex's dark eyes as she gathered the fine silk about her.

His lips had parted, as if he was about to say something but the words had frozen on his tongue. His stare intensified, dropping to the pinpoints of her nipples where they peaked against the soft blush-colored fabric. Her breath caught in her throat, she could almost feel his gaze as if it was a touch against her skin.

She shifted on the bed, untangling her legs and pushing them over the side of the mattress, the movement making her robe slide across her nakedness like a caress. Heat built everywhere—her cheeks, her chest and deeper darker places she didn't want to acknowledge with Alex standing there, staring hungrily at her as if she was to be his appetizer before the evening meal.

"Alex?" Loren asked, finally getting to her feet and welcoming the feel of her robe settling like a cloak about her, hiding her.

"Okay, five minutes. Come out onto the terrace."

He pushed one hand through his hair, the vulnerability of that action striking her square in the chest, before turning for the staircase leading back up to the main floor. Loren took a steadying breath. She hadn't meant to fall asleep but weariness had dragged at every inch of her body. To be woken by him had reminded her starkly of the day she'd arrived at the castillo. Of how he'd kissed the palm of her hand, of how she'd believed their marriage to be so full of promise at that moment.

Even now, her body still thrummed in reaction to Alex's presence, and he hadn't so much as touched her this time. It had only been a look, but it had set her senses on fire despite how angry she was with both him and herself for the debacle they now found themselves in.

Coming here had been a terrible idea. She should have resisted. Should have demanded he take her back to the castillo. She could have avoided him there for most of the time at least. Thrown herself into her duties as patroness of the orphanage. Something. Anything but time in this isolated beauty alone together.

Loren spun on her bare foot and skittered across the floor to where she'd found her suitcase. She hadn't bothered to check its contents before her shower, only grabbing at the first thing she could find at the time, her robe. But now she wondered just what she had to wear. She certainly hoped her maid had covered all possibilities.

She flipped open the lid of the case and rummaged through the layers of swimwear with matching wraps and night wear Bella had packed for her, tossing it all to one side. Finally, thankfully, her fingers closed around some basic cotton T-shirts. Loren lifted them out and put them on the bed behind her before searching through her case again. A small gasp of relief escaped her as she found a batik wraparound skirt her mother had brought back for her from Indonesia a couple of years ago.

All she needed now was clean underwear. Loren pulled open a drawer of the dresser in her room and swiftly put away the things she'd already taken from the case, then methodically unpacked the rest—her frustration rising by degrees until the case was completely empty.

What on earth had her maid been thinking? No underwear? Not even a pair of cotton panties? She prayed that Bella had perhaps run out of room in her case and had packed her underthings with Alex's, but a rapid check of his room showed no sign of anything of hers.

The chime of a clock upstairs reminded her that she'd told Alex she'd only be five minutes. Sliding her robe off, Loren picked up the underwear she'd worn all day. The idea of wearing them again, against clean skin, just felt wrong. She'd have to make sure she rinsed them out before bed tonight and bought some more lingerie tomorrow.

Loren chose the thickest of her T-shirts and pulled it on, then swiftly wrapped the skirt about her waist and slid her feet into flat leather mules.

The cotton of the batik skirt was soft against her buttocks and she was acutely conscious of the brush of fabric caressing her bare skin as she walked up the stairs. Maybe going commando hadn't been such a clever idea after all.

Out on the terrace Alex had set a small round table with a clutch of flowers and had lit a large squat candle that flickered in the gentle evening breeze. Knives, forks and two colorful serviettes completed the setting.

"I'll have to buy you a watch, I think," Alex said as

he walked toward her holding a flute of champagne in each hand.

Loren took one and smiled in return. Not for anything would she admit what had delayed her.

"I thought it was a woman's prerogative to be late."

"When she is as lovely as you, then she's always worth waiting for."

"Even ten years?"

Loren couldn't help it. The words had popped into her mind and past her lips before she could think. Alex tipped the rim of his glass against hers.

"Especially then," he said, a tone to his voice she couldn't quite put her finger on. "To a better beginning, hmm?"

"If you say so," she replied, and took a long delicious sip of the bubbling golden liquid.

She was certain the alcohol bypassed her stomach and went straight to her legs, because all of a sudden they felt tingly, the muscles weak.

"I think I'd better have something to eat. That feels as if it'll have me on my ear if I keep it up."

"Here, try the antipasto."

Alex crossed the few short steps to a stone bench next to the outdoor grill. He picked up a platter and offered it to her, watching again with those velvet black eyes as she selected a sliver of artichoke heart and popped it into her mouth.

"How is that?" he asked as she chewed and swallowed.

"Good. Here, try some."

Without thinking, Loren picked up another piece and proffered it to him. He paused a moment before opening his lips. She held the morsel, startled as his lips closed around the tips of her fingers, their moist warmth and softness sending a jolt of need rocketing down her arm.

"You're right," Alex said after he'd swallowed and taken another sip of wine. "That was very good. Give me something else."

Her hand shook slightly as she chose a stuffed olive and held it before him. He bent his head and slowly took the fruit into his mouth, his tongue hotly sweeping between the pads of her forefinger and thumb as he did so. If she'd thought the wine had made her legs weak, the caress of his tongue made them doubly so.

"Don't!" she cried.

"Don't do what?"

"That. What you just did. Just...don't."

"It disturbs you, my touch?"

Oh, far more than he could ever imagine, but she certainly wasn't going to let him know that painful truth.

"No, I just don't like it. That's all. Here, let me put the platter on the table, then we can help ourselves."

Loren relieved him of the platter and set it on the table next to the candle then settled herself on one of the wrought iron chairs before her legs gave way completely.

The warmth of the sun-heated metal seeped through the thin cotton of her skirt—heating other, more sensitive places. Loren shifted slightly but the motion only enhanced the sensation.

"Uncomfortable out here? Perhaps you'd rather sit indoors," Alex suggested as he topped off their glasses before sitting down opposite her.

"No, it's okay. I'm fine," Loren assured him, all the while forcing her body to relax.

Maybe it was the wine, or perhaps it was merely the

exquisitely beautiful setting, but Loren felt herself begin to relax by degrees. By the time Alex rose to bake fillets of fish, garnished with herbs and lemon and wrapped in foil, on the outdoor grill she was feeling decidedly mellow. She rose from the table and took the near-empty antipasto platter through to the kitchen indoors.

The kitchen was very compact and narrow—a long row of cupboards down one side and the bench top and stove running parallel, with little more than a few feet between them. Loren searched the cupboards for a small dish to put the leftover antipasto into, and then the drawers for some cling wrap to cover it. She'd found a space for the dish in the heavily stocked fridge and was just about to rinse off the platter when Alex came through from the terrace.

He squeezed behind her, far more closely than necessary, she decided with a ripple of irritation.

"The fish is just about done. Can you grab the salad from the fridge? I'll get our plates."

He was so close his breath stirred the hair against the nape of her neck. She could feel the solid heat of his body as he pressed up against her buttocks and reached past her to grab the jug of vinaigrette dressing from the bench top.

She would not react to him; she would not. Loren clenched her hands into fists on the countertop, fighting against the urge to allow her body to lean back into the strength of his. It was almost a physical impossibility in the close confines of the kitchen.

Thankfully, Alex appeared to be oblivious to the racing emotions that swirled inside her. He propped the jug on top of the two dinner plates he'd taken from the crockery pantry behind her and was already on his way back outside.

She took a deep steadying breath before opening the fridge again and lifting out the bowl of salad he'd obviously prepared while she slept. The crisp salad greens, interspersed with feta, olives and succulent freshly cut tomatoes looked mouthwateringly tempting, but nowhere near as appetizing as the man who was currently walking away from her.

No matter how idyllic this setting, the next two weeks would be absolute hell on earth.

Eight

To her surprise, over the next few days, Loren began to relax in a way she hadn't managed in some time. Yet beneath the surface a simmering tension lay between her and Alex.

As yet, he'd made no overtures to force their relationship onto a physical level. By day she was eternally grateful for that, but every night as she lay tangled in her sheets aching for the man who slept only a corridor width away from her room, she wondered whether she had indeed made the right decision in denying him her body.

He lied to you, she reminded herself. *He appealed to you on an emotional level he knew you could not refuse. He manipulated you for his own ends.*

But he hadn't done so for personal gain, she argued back silently as the moon traversed the sky and she wriggled against her mattress and stared out through the glass doors that led onto a small balcony off her room. He'd done it for his grandfather, to assuage the old man's sudden and irrational fears about the family's longevity.

It doesn't matter, she argued back again, thumping her pillow in frustration as she tried to get comfortable. He should have told her the truth from the start. How on earth did he expect to embark upon a marriage without even honesty between them? Without truth, they had nothing, because they certainly didn't have love. At least, not a love that was reciprocated.

Giving up on sleep, Loren rose from her bed and walked over to the French doors. She pushed them open and stepped out onto the balcony. The night air was balmy and still, enveloping her in a myriad of scents and sounds. She looked up at the clear night sky, observing the constellations so different to how they appeared back in New Zealand, and suddenly she was struck with a sense of loneliness that brought sudden tears to her eyes.

A tiny sob pushed up from her chest and ejected into the darkness. She gripped the iron balcony railing tight beneath her hands, but no matter how hard she squeezed she could not stop the flow of tears down her cheeks.

This wasn't how she imagined her life would be. She'd expected happiness. A mutual respect between herself and Alex. Respect that would hopefully grow to become more. Loren dragged a shaking breath into her aching lungs and blinked against the moisture that continued to well in her eyes. It seemed that now she'd started to cry, she was incapable of stopping.

The air beside her shifted and she turned her head to see Alex standing on the balcony beside her. Wearing only a pair of silken pajama pants, he looked like some god risen from the sea in the moonlight. Silver beams caressed the muscled width of his chest and shoulders, throwing the lean, defined strength into shadowed relief.

"What's wrong?"

"I…" Loren shook her head, averting her eyes, both unwilling and unable to verbalize what ailed her.

Warm, strong arms closed around her in comfort, drawing her against the smooth plane of his chest.

At first she resisted—she didn't trust him, she couldn't—but his arms tightened around her and for just that moment she wanted to forget all her dashed hopes and give in to his silent support. She let her cheek settle against his chest, her gulped sobs calming as her breathing adjusted to his, her heartbeat slowing to his strong steady rhythm.

She felt Alex's chin drop to the top of her head, felt the slight tug of the bristles of his beard in her hair. She nestled in closer, relishing the feel of his body against hers. His masculine form felt unfamiliar to her and yet instantly recognizable—as if this was where she had belonged all her life, safe within the circle of his arms.

Fresh tears sprang to her eyes at the foolishly irrational thought. She may have thought she belonged with him, but the truth couldn't be more converse.

"Hush, Loren," he whispered against her hair. "We will work this out."

"I don't think we can, Alex."

"One way or another, we will work it out."

With a powerful sweep of muscle, Alex lifted her into his arms and took her back into her room. Still holding her to him he settled onto the mattress and leaned back against the padded headrest. Loren's head rested against his shoulder, her legs across his lap. She struggled to sit up and tried to push him away. With her defenses as weak as they were right now she couldn't afford to give him any leeway.

"Relax, I'm not going to try and force you into anything. You're upset. Let me comfort you."

She hesitated a moment before allowing the slow circular motion of his hand across her back to soothe her. Eventually her eyes slid closed and she allowed her senses to be filled with the gentleness of his touch, the steadiness of his breathing and the delicious warmth and scent of his bare skin.

Alex felt Loren relax by degrees until she finally drifted back off into sleep. Inside, his thoughts were in turmoil. Each day that passed saw them spending practically every waking moment together, yet each day she seemed to withdraw from him more and more. So much so that tonight she hadn't even felt as if she could accept his comfort.

Ironically, that had hurt more than the days they'd spent together so far, where he'd fought to keep his libido firmly under control, and far more than the nights where he'd lain on his bed, wondering if a quick dip in the Adriatic Sea would help diminish the fire raging under his skin.

He remembered back to a time when she'd been just a toddler. Her parents had been visiting his and for one reason or another she'd taken a tumble. Rather than seek consolation from either her father or mother, she'd tottered toward him, past them both, and offered her grazed palms for his inspection and reassurance that she was okay.

His brothers had teased him mercilessly. He'd been all

of ten or eleven years old and they'd thought it hilarious that Loren had come to him. But now, in the moonlit night, with her slumbering in his arms, he remembered how it had secretly made him feel. Remembered the sense of responsibility and duty he had to protect her and keep her safe from all harm.

And here he was now, having harmed her in the worst way possible. He'd betrayed her trust and brought her back to a world that was no longer familiar to her, to people whose only memories of her were as a child and not as a woman with hopes and dreams of her own.

Anger curled a tight fist deep in his gut. He should never have interrupted her life. Never have brought her back. She'd had a new world in New Zealand yet she'd eschewed all of that to return to the old one she'd left behind. For him. He owed it to her to somehow make up for that wrong.

He knew that he still had to fulfill his duty to his grandfather and the people of Isla Sagrado. But for the first time, he admitted to himself that duty to family extended beyond his brothers and *Abuelo*. He was a married man now. His wife came first.

Bright bursts of morning light stabbed at Loren's eyes, dragging her to full consciousness. Beneath her, her bed had grown increasingly lumpy as she stretched and squirmed awake.

Lumpy? Realization and remembrance dawned with a rush. That lump was her husband; in fact, it was one particular part of her husband. Sometime during the night Alex had slid them both down onto the mattress and, as unaccustomed as she was to sharing a bed with anyone—let alone her husband—Loren had remained sprawled halfway across his body.

Even now the delicious scent of his skin, that blend of spice and citrus tang combined with the heat of his own special smell, teased at her nostrils and warmed her in places that made her squirm again.

"Loren, you will have to stop doing that or I cannot be answerable for my actions."

"Oh!" she exclaimed, springing away from him as if he'd delivered a high-voltage current directly to her.

She jumped up off the bed and kept her eyes averted from his prone form, from the irrefutable evidence that her actions had not left him unaffected.

"I'm sorry, I didn't mean to."

Alex sighed. She heard him stretch on the sheets and fought the urge to turn her eyes to him, to drink in the sight of his male beauty.

"Yes, I am sure you didn't mean to."

He sounded so tired and a pang of remorse plucked at her conscience. He'd come to her in the night when she was at her most vulnerable and he'd offered solace. No questions asked.

"I'm sorry, Alex. Truly. And I…" She pressed her lips together, looking for the right words. "Thank you for last night."

"*De nada*. It is what couples do, after all, is it not? Offer one another ease?"

Her eyes flew to his. She hadn't misunderstood the double entendre in his remark if the look on his face was anything to go by.

"Yes, well, I appreciate it." She shifted her weight from one foot to the other, unsure of what else to say or do.

"Go and have your shower, Loren. You are perfectly safe walking past me. As I said last night, I am not going to force you into anything."

"Anything else, you mean."

Alex sat up and swung his legs over the side of the bed. He stood and Loren's gaze was inexorably drawn to his torso, to his taut stomach and the fine scattering of dark hair that arrowed down from his belly button to the waistband of his pajama pants.

There was a thread of steel in his voice when he spoke, a thread that warned he was barely holding on to his temper.

"Remarks like that are unbecoming to a woman of your intelligence. Whatever my sins, I did not force you into marrying me."

Loren dropped her head in shame. He was right. She had to stop treating him as if he was solely to blame for their position. He made a sound of disgust and she heard him walk past her and leave the room, his own bedroom door slamming shut behind him.

She should apologize. Before she could change her mind, Loren followed him and knocked tentatively on his door. At his response she slowly opened it and stepped inside.

"I shouldn't have said what I did. I'm sorry."

Alex gave her a hard look but the small frown lines that bracketed his mouth eased a little. He gave her a small nod.

"Apology accepted."

"Thank you." Unsure of what to do next, Loren started to close the door again. "I'll leave you to get dressed."

"Loren?"

"Yes?"

"I am not such an ogre, you know. I am merely a man. A man with responsibilities and needs."

There was something in the tone of his voice that

spoke of a deep-seated longing that struck straight to her core. She felt the inexorable pull of it even as she started to move across the room.

He stood still and watched her as she came toward him, his stance proud. There was a frankness in his eyes that spoke straight to Loren's heart. In all of this she hadn't stopped to consider what this marriage had cost him. He hadn't married her for his own gain but for that of the people of Isla Sagrado and for the sake of his grandfather's fears. Whether Alex himself believed in the curse was irrelevant. He'd married her out of his respect and love for *Abuelo* and in determination to do whatever it took to lift the spirits of the people who looked to the del Castillo family for so much.

Loren lifted one hand and raised it to Alex's cheek, her fingers gently cupping his whisker-rough skin. She slowly rose on her tiptoes and pressed her lips to his. Softly, shyly, she kissed him. To her chagrin, his lips remained unresponsive beneath hers. Uncertain, she started to pull her hand away, but Alex's hand shot up to hold it there and to press it against his face, his long fingers covering hers.

"Don't play with me, Loren. Even I have limits."

"I…I'm not playing, Alex."

She reached up to kiss him again, this time feeling a zing of power as she felt his lips tremble beneath hers. She traced the seam of his mouth with the tip of her tongue, feeling suddenly bolder than she'd ever felt before. He was a man who had everything and wanted for nothing. This was all she could give him. Her love.

Alex's arms wrapped around her, pulling her against his hard male form, showing her in no uncertain terms that he was more than prepared to accept what she offered. Loren stroked her hands across his shoulders, loving the feel of his leashed strength beneath her fingertips. His body burned into hers, making the light summer tank top and cotton shorts she'd worn to bed feel as if they were too much against her skin.

She strained against him, wanting more, yet not quite fully understanding what it was she needed. Alex's strong hands skimmed down her back and over the mounds of her buttocks, cupping them and pulling her up higher against him. Angling the part of her body that ached with a demanding throb against his arousal. A shock of pleasure radiated through her at the pressure of his sex against her. She felt herself grow damp and hot.

He pulled her to him again and flexed his hips against her, starting a rhythm that made her whole body pulse with need. Loren slid her hands up the cords of his neck and knotted her fingers in his short dark hair, pulling his face down to hers, wanting to absorb every part of him any way she could.

"Lift your legs and put them around my waist," Alex commanded, his voice vibrating with desire.

Through the haze of passion that focused her senses only on the touch and taste of the man in her arms, she managed to comply. Alex walked them to the bed and laid her down on the sheets, still rumpled from last night. Without losing physical contact, he lay down with her, their bodies aligning perfectly, his legs cradled between hers.

Loren's breasts ached and swelled against the soft cotton of her top, her nipples pressing like twin points against Alex's chest. At this moment she hated the barrier that stood between them. As if he read her mind, Alex shifted his weight slightly, then his hands were at the hem of her top, pushing it up and over her head and exposing her small round breasts with their blush-colored peaks.

"So perfect," he murmured as he traced the outline of first one dusky pink nipple, then the other, with the tip of his finger.

She watched, unable to speak, unable to move, as he moistened his finger with his tongue then retraced the shape of her again. A shudder rippled through her, bringing a small smile of intent to Alex's face. Then he brought his lips to a tight bud, his tongue flicking out to mimic what his finger had been doing only seconds before.

Another shudder spread through her body, this one bringing a swell of pleasure with it, a swell that ballooned as Alex's lips closed over her nipple and sucked hard. She nearly leapt off the bed, her body arching into him, wanting all he could give her. His hips held her pinned against the mattress and she hooked her legs around his, running her feet over his calves, the slippery fabric of his pajamas soft and sensual against her soles.

His body felt so different from her own. Stronger, firmer and with an energy vibrating from deep inside of him that excited her both mentally and physically. She knew what was yet to come, knew that there would be discomfort, possibly even pain, but she also knew to the depths of her soul that this was totally right. That out of anyone, Alex was the only man she could ever be this intimate with.

She gasped aloud as he scraped his teeth over her nipple before lavishing more of the same attention to its twin. She thought she would go mad with the sensations he wrung from her body. He was trailing his tongue along the curve of her breast, sending a rash of goose bumps to pepper her skin as, one by one, he traced each rib, lower and lower.

Despite the warm air she felt a shiver flow across her skin. His hands were at the drawstring tie of her shorts, she felt the bow loosen, the fabric begin to give way. Alex pulled himself up onto his knees and tugged her shorts away from her, exposing her body's deepest intimacy to his scorching gaze.

She felt wanton under the power of his stare and she squirmed against the sheets, relishing the feel of high-thread-count cotton softness against the bare skin of her buttocks. Her movement caused a flush to deepen high on Alex's cheekbones, made his eyes darken even more. He reached for her, his broad hands holding her hips firmly, his fingers splayed across her skin as he lowered his face to the V at the apex of her thighs.

Loren tensed, unsure of what to expect. All tension flowed from her as he pressed his lips with unerring accuracy at the central spot that was the heart of the sensations pouring through her. She felt his tongue gently glide over her sensitized nerves and lost all sense of reality. Again and again his tongue swept over her, gentle at first then firmer until, when she thought she could bear it no longer, he closed his mouth over that spot and suckled as he had done with her nipples only moments ago.

Sensation splintered through her body, at first sharp and then in increasing undulating waves of sheer pleasure reaching a crescendo of feeling she'd never dreamed herself capable of. Her entire body tensed, taut like a bow, before she collapsed back against the bed, weak, spent. Sated.

She sensed Alex's movement, heard the slither of

fabric as he shucked off his pajama bottoms. She opened her eyes as he knelt between her splayed legs, watched as he stroked his hand from base to tip of his erection. He positioned himself at her entrance and she felt the hot, blunt probe of his flesh.

A sudden shaft of fear shot through her. "I haven't… I mean, I've never…"

"Shh," Alex said soothingly. "I know. I will take care of you, Loren. Trust me."

She locked her gaze with his, searching for any hint that he could be untrue to her, even now as they lay together with nothing but their past between them.

"I do. I trust you, Alex," she whispered.

"That's my girl," he replied.

He leaned down and kissed her, his tongue sweeping inside her mouth to tangle with hers. She welcomed his invasion, letting her senses focus on the thrust and parry of his kiss, and the blend of her essence and the flavor that was all his.

She felt his hips slowly push against hers, felt him slide within her body. She stiffened involuntarily, unsure how she would accommodate him, but then he withdrew and did the same thing again, this time probing a little farther, waiting a little longer. Her body stretched and molded around him, at first uncomfortable and then not. Tremors racked his frame as he held himself partially within her. The next time he moved, she pressed back, taking him inside her a little farther.

A new sensation began to build inside her, one that demanded more, demanded him, so much so that when he thrust all the way inside her on his next stroke she ignored the sharp tear of pain and clutched at his hips, urging him to continue. With no barrier impeding him, Alex deepened his strokes, propelling her once more toward the growing pleasure whose epicenter lay hidden within her.

He gathered momentum and Loren found her body meeting him stroke for stroke, both of them reaching for the shadowy pinnacle of their desire. And then it burst upon her. Wave after wave. Bigger than before, deeper than before. A cry of sheer delight broke on her lips as Alex shuddered in release against her, before collapsing, spent, against her body.

In the aftermath of their lovemaking Loren gave herself over to the delicious lassitude that spread through her body. She knew of physical pleasure, but she'd never dreamed it could be like this. She trailed her fingers up and down the length of Alex's sweat-dampened spine and in that moment she loved him more than she ever had before.

Alex watched his wife as she slept naked in his arms. His heart still hammered in his chest. Coming down from the high of their first physical union had taken its time. Even now he still felt twinges of pleasure, aftershocks of satisfaction that seemed endless in their reach.

It had never been like this before, with anyone. Somehow the knowledge that he was Loren's husband and her first lover had lent a different note to the act itself. He'd always prided himself on being a considerate lover but it had become even more important to him to ensure that her first time be special than he'd believed possible.

And in giving he'd also received. The climax that had wrung his body dry had been spectacular. He rested one hand on her smooth, flat belly. Perhaps even now he'd managed to achieve his goal.

He had scarcely been able to believe his luck when she'd followed him to his room. After last night he'd hoped they'd gained a new high ground together, but her reaction to him this morning had dashed that hope. Until he'd heard that gentle knock at his bedroom door.

Alex dropped his head back against the pillow. He'd made that first time special for her. No matter what came after, she would always have that. Somehow that truth didn't help assuage the kernel of guilt that had nestled somewhere in his chest. She deserved to have her first time with someone who loved her. But whatever she deserved, Alex was what she had—what she *would* have for the rest of her life, since he had no intention of ever letting her go.

She stirred against him, her slender body curling around his as naturally as if they'd always slept together. He'd had enough of thinking, enough of trying to justify his decisions. Action came more naturally.

Pushing aside thoughts that could only plague him, Alex gathered Loren closer to him and began to stroke her with long sweeps of his hand. He was already hard for her again. Mindful that she might be tender, he decided this time to take things even slower.

She woke as he dragged his fingertips along the inner curve of her hip. A tremulous smile pulled at her lips, soon to be lost in a moan that tore from her throat as he slid one hand between her legs to gently stroke her soft folds.

"Too much? Too soon?" he asked, watching her face carefully, hoping against hope that she would say no to his inquiry.

"Oh!" she cried as he brushed over her clitoris. "No, not too much. Not too soon."

"Good." He smiled in return and focused on the task at hand.

She had so much still to learn about the pleasure they could give one another, and he thanked his lucky stars she was such an eager pupil.

Her legs began to quake in what he recognized as the precursor to her climax and he slowed his touch, drawing out the pleasure for her as far as he was able. When he himself could hold on no longer he pulled her beneath him and sank inside her, the action sending her skyrocketing over the edge. Just like that he was with her, his body pulsing, spilling his seed, his mind filled with nothing more than wave after wave of ecstasy and the overwhelming sense of rightness that consumed him with Loren in his arms.

Nine

While Loren loved living at the castillo she adored the compactness of this stone cottage perched on the hillside. The small kitchen that had so tormented her with its closeness when she and Alex had first arrived was now a teasing adventure. And, even though they had neighbors in abundance, with the mature trees and the staggered terrace style of building around them, she felt as if she and Alex were totally isolated. There was a delightful sense of freedom in knowing that she could do whatever she wished.

It had been one glorious week since the morning they'd first made love. A week filled with discovery as she'd learned to bring the strong man she'd married exquisite physical delight and receive the same in return. Her one regret was that while they grew closer physically with each encounter, Alex continued to maintain an emotional distance between them she couldn't seem to break through.

They'd done all the tourist things available in the area, enjoying the food and the countryside almost as much as they enjoyed one another in the close confines of the cottage. Going back to the castillo would be difficult but she had very definite plans for her and Alex to plan more time alone together.

A smile pulled at her lips as she heard Alex come up the stairs from the pebble beach below where they'd been swimming together. Only the knowledge that they'd been visible to some of their neighbors while in the water had held them back from making love as they'd floated together. But now, her smile deepened, now they were in their own cocoon of privacy again and she could do what she wished.

Alex lowered his body onto one of the sun loungers on the terrace, the white-and-navy striped cushion beneath him accenting the depth of his tan. Black swim trunks clung to him, outlining his hips and the tops of his thighs. Loren's mouth watered at the prospect of what lay hidden beneath the dark fabric.

Her hands gripped the edges of the tray she'd brought through from the kitchen and she put it down on the terrace table, none too gently, and grabbed at one of the highball glasses before it toppled over. Even after all they'd shared he continued to have the power to rattle her senses. Just thinking about him had her heart racing, her lower body flushed and eager for his touch.

She forced her hands to still so she could grab the pitcher of iced tea and pour two glasses. She took one over to Alex, aware of his eyes watching every step she took toward him.

"Cool drink?" she said, offering him a glass.

"After that swim I think I need more than a cool drink."

He took the proffered drink and drained the glass with a series of long, slow pulls. Loren watched, mesmerized by the play of muscles working in his throat. Alex put his glass down on the terrace beside him, the unmelted blocks of ice tinkling in the bottom, and gestured to Loren to join him on the lounger.

"Here, come and sit with me."

"There's no room," Loren half protested.

"So use your imagination." Alex smiled in return.

Loren lifted the folds of the emerald green sarong that matched her bikini and straddled the lounger, settling on Alex's strong thighs.

"Like this?" she said, her voice a husky rasp as she felt the hairs on his legs tickle the already sensitive flesh of her inner thighs.

"Oh yes, exactly like that."

Alex pushed the flimsy sarong aside, baring her legs completely and exposing the shadowed area of her body at the apex of her thighs. He traced the outside edge of her bikini bottoms, from the tie at her hip to her inner thigh and back again.

Heat and moisture flooded to her lower regions and she drew in a sharp breath as one finger slipped inside the edge of her bikini pants to brush lightly over her inner folds. Back and forth he stroked, until finally he slid one finger inside her. She clenched her inner muscles against him, tilting her pelvis forward and rocking slightly against his palm.

"You like that?" he asked, his voice deep and low.

"You know I do," she whispered back and gasped anew as he slid another finger inside her.

With his free hand, Alex tugged at the bows that held

her bikini bottoms together and pulled the fabric away, dropping it beside the lounger, exposing her and what he was doing to her.

Loren looked down and felt another sharp jolt of pleasure rock through her body as she watched him. She ached for release, wanted to rush toward the starburst of pleasure she knew was just around the corner, yet conversely wanted to make it last as long as she could. When Alex's thumb settled against the hooded bud of nerve endings at her core she nearly lost it, but she clenched against him, harder, tighter, determined to remain in control.

"Come for me," Alex commanded, his voice guttural now, his eyes molten with desire.

He started a gentle circular motion with his thumb, slowly increasing and releasing pressure with each stroke. She was near mindless when she felt the first flutters of her orgasm begin to wash over her. Finally, she could hold back no more. She tilted her hips some more, leaning into his hand, and let his magical touch send her flying over the edge.

Loren slowly returned to her surroundings, to the man who lay beneath her. A beautiful sensual smile pulled at his lips and she felt herself smile back in return.

"You're beautiful when you climax, did you know that?" he said.

Loren felt the heat of a blush stain her cheeks. Even after what they'd just done she still felt embarrassed when he spoke to her like that. In lieu of a response she leaned forward and captured his lips with hers. He tasted of a delicious combination of sunshine, tea and a hint of mint.

She broke off the kiss and pulled free from his arms.

"It seems to me that things are a little unbalanced here," she said.

"Unbalanced?"

Loren traced the prominent outline of his erection through his swim trunks with her fingernails.

"You heard me."

"Hmm, you could be right," Alex said, his speech thickening as she continued to tease his length. "It's always important for things to be balanced, of course."

"I was thinking the exact same thing," Loren said and rose from the lounger in a fluid movement.

She undid the knot of her sarong and let it drop to the terrace floor, and then undid her bikini top, allowing it to fall on top of the puddle of emerald green fabric. Her nipples tightened in anticipation in spite of the warm air as she bent toward her husband.

"Lift your hips," she said.

As he did, she eased his trunks down, exposing him to her hungry gaze and her eager hands. She tossed the shorts behind her, uncaring of where they fell.

"Now, spread your legs," she requested. She knelt between them on the striped cushion as he silently obeyed.

Loren leaned forward and took his erection in her hand, curling her fingers around the velvet hard length and stroking firmly from base to tip and back again. Bending down, she swirled her tongue around the tip of him. Again and again, before gently rasping her teeth over the smooth head. She smiled as a harsh groan tore from Alex's lips.

"Too much? Do you want me to stop?" she teased. She knew what his answer would be before he could even verbalize it.

"Stop now and I may have to punish you severely," Alex said through gritted teeth.

Loren laughed softly and took him in her mouth. She loved that she could do this to him, for him. Just a few months ago, she would never have dreamed she could be so bold, so forward, but he'd taught her much in this past week. Most importantly, he'd taught her how to give him pleasure and how to draw that pleasure out until he finally let go of the iron control with which he held himself.

She looked up at his face. His head was thrown back against the chair cushion, his eyes squeezed closed. He'd flung his arms back and his hands gripped the back of the lounger. Loren took him deeper into her mouth, suckled more firmly at his tip, relished the hot salty taste of him as he fought to hold back.

Then she stopped, releasing him to the warm air around them. Alex tilted his head back up, his eyes narrowed as he watched her rise and spread her legs before lowering herself back down. She guided his shaft to her with unerring accuracy.

His hands let go of the lounger, finding a new home cupping her breasts as she took his length inside her body. She leaned against the strength of his arms as she started a rhythm guaranteed to bring them both to completion. Beneath her she could feel Alex's body tremble with the sheer force of his indomitable will. She knew he would not allow himself the freedom of his climax unless he knew she too was near.

But this time she wanted to drive him over the edge. This time she wanted to show him that love was not all about control or always about giving. Sometimes it was about taking what you needed, when it was offered.

And she was offering herself. Everything. Her heart, her body, her soul.

She knew the second she'd overcome his resistance. Felt the moment his body began to let go. Intense joy flooded her mind. Hard on the heels of that sense of elation, her own orgasm shuddered through her.

Loren collapsed against Alex's body, both of them slicked with sweat, and lay against his chest, listening to the rapid thud of his heartbeat.

"I love you, Alexander del Castillo," she whispered.

In answer he wrapped his arms around her and pulled her even closer—but the words she wished to hear, more than any other from his mouth, remained unsaid.

They'd been back from Dubrovnik for nearly a week. Already their time together seemed as if it was a distant memory. Alex had disappeared back into his work as if nothing else existed. Apparently bookings at the resort were on the increase. The publicity surrounding their marriage had seemed to have done the trick as far as lifting the profile of Isla Sagrado in the media. Once again the island nation was becoming a popular holiday destination for the moneyed and famous.

Loren was pleased for Alex that things were improving so steadily although she sometimes wished the demands of his work were less so they could recapture some of the wonder of their honeymoon again. It was rare that Alex arrived home before she went to bed anymore, and he hadn't been to her room or in her bed since their first night back.

She'd believed they'd built a foundation for their future together in those exquisite days and nights at the cottage, yet now she was no longer so certain. This morning a courier had delivered her a copy of their prenuptial agreement for her records. It served as a sobering reminder of the parameters under which she and Alex had married.

Had he encouraged their intimacy, their discovery of one another, purely to make the child he was so determined to produce? Before the wedding, he'd gone with her to the doctor where she'd had a physical check and the doctor had discussed her cycle. Alex had known when she should have been most fertile. That that time had coincided so soon after their wedding was fortuitous, he'd said, as they'd driven back from the clinic.

Was that why he'd been so patient with her? So passionate? Had making a baby been the sole object of their lovemaking?

Her period had been due a few days ago but as yet hadn't made its appearance. She placed a hand on her stomach, wondering if Alex would have his wish after all. As much as she desired to bear his child, she wanted more from their marriage before she felt ready to bring a child into it. Especially now she knew just what it would be like to share a life with him.

Unless, of course, their honeymoon had been a farce—nothing but a means to an end for Alex.

"Señora?"

Loren turned from the flowers she'd been arranging for the dining table tonight and greeted the maid who'd brought a cordless phone on a silver tray.

"A call for me?" she said, picking up the handset.

"Sí, it is *Señor* del Castillo."

Loren felt an instant rush of elation and hit the hold button, saying "hello" before the maid had even left the room.

"Loren, I left some papers in my office at home and I can't spare Giselle to come to the castillo to collect them. Would you be able to bring them to the resort?"

Hard on the heels of disappointment that he didn't so much as ask how she was feeling, she found herself agreeing to do so.

"Sure, I can do that. I'm expected at the orphanage at lunchtime for a concert with the children. I can stop in to your office on my way through."

"Thanks, I appreciate it. You'll find them in the blue folder on my desk."

Without waiting for her to say goodbye, Alex disconnected the call. He'd treated her as no more than one of his staff. Loren felt a bubble of anger rise in her throat. Anger mixed with another emotion she didn't want to examine too closely for fear it would bring her to tears.

She swallowed hard against the obstruction in her throat and squared her shoulders. She would tell him what she thought of his manner when she saw him. If he thought he could treat her like that and get away with it, well, he had another think coming.

Half an hour later Loren drove her new Alfa Romeo Spider—a belated wedding gift surprise from Alex when they'd arrived home—toward the resort's main offices and pulled into the visitor parking lot outside. She looked around for Alex's Lamborghini but it was nowhere to be seen. Strange, but then perhaps he'd used a driver today.

She collected the blue folder he'd requested from the passenger seat and walked with clipped, sure steps toward the office door. Inside, with a wave to the receptionist, Loren made her way directly to Alex's office.

Even as hurt and angry as she was, her heart lifted at the prospect of seeing him like this in the middle of the day. Perhaps she'd even be able to persuade him to come with her to the lunchtime concert.

Her hopes were dashed, however, as she was greeted by Giselle at Alex's office door.

"Oh, thanks. You finally brought them, did you?" Giselle said, unfolding her elegant long legs from behind her desk and coming to relieve Loren of the folder.

"I'd like to give this directly to Alex myself, if you don't mind," Loren stated, holding firmly on to the cardboard packet.

"Oh, he's not here."

"He's not? Where—"

"Didn't he tell you? Of course, obviously not. He had a meeting in Puerto Seguro with some potential investors for the resort expansion. I'll take these with me as I'm headed that way now."

Loren let go of the documents. As she did so she was assailed with a sense of dizziness. Giselle was quick to react, putting a hand under Loren's elbow and guiding her to sit on a large sofa against one wall.

"Are you okay?" Giselle asked. "You've gone awfully pale."

"It's nothing. I skipped breakfast this morning and I shouldn't have."

"Are you sure that's all it is? After all, Alex is a very—" Giselle paused for a moment, her face suddenly reflective "—virile man. And you've just had a couple of weeks at the cottage in Dubrovnik, yes? It's so beautiful there. So deliciously private and romantic, don't you think?"

Giselle spoke so knowingly—indeed, with such familiarity—that nausea pitched through Loren's body.

Oblivious to Loren's discomfort, the other woman continued.

"Alex will be pleased if you've fallen pregnant so soon." She patted Loren's hand. "That would mean he'd be able to go back to normal so much sooner than he'd planned."

What exactly was Giselle referring to? It wasn't as if subtlety was the woman's strong point. She had to be referring to Alex and her resuming their relationship.

"Back to normal?" Loren asked, hoping against hope that her suspicions were ridiculous.

"I'm sure you know exactly what I mean." Giselle smiled in return but there was little humor in the cold glitter of her eyes. Instead, the proprietary nature of the curve of her lips said it all.

"Oh, dear, look at the time. I'd better get these to Alex before he comes bellowing on the phone, demanding to know where I am. I'll let you see yourself out. You look as though you could do with a few minutes to yourself."

Within seconds Loren was left alone with nothing but the slightly cloying scent of Giselle's perfume in the air around her.

She shook her head slowly. No. What Giselle had said couldn't be true. Go back to his old life and ways? Alex wasn't that kind of man, surely. Not the Alex she thought she knew, anyway. Before their marriage his playboy lifestyle had been well represented in the media, but months before he'd come to New Zealand he'd all but dropped out of circulation. She'd noted it at the time, long before she'd had any reason to believe his new and uncharacteristic circumspection might have anything to do with her.

Loren leaned against the big square cushion of the

couch. Had it all been part of his carefully orchestrated plan to prove to everyone that he could break the curse? Even *Abuelo* would have had a hard time believing that Alex would have gone directly from playboy bachelorhood to married. But what would happen now? Once their PR campaign of a marriage had served its purpose and they'd fulfilled the terms of the prenuptial agreement, would Alex revert back to his old social life, leaving her to sit at home with the children?

Children? Oh, Lord. What if she *was* pregnant? There was no way she'd raise a child here with him if he was going to have affairs behind her back—or even in front of her, if it came to that.

One thing was certain, Loren thought. If she was pregnant, Alex would be the last person she'd be telling until she knew exactly what kind of father he planned to be.

Ten

Loren had a pounding headache by the time she left the orphanage after the children's concert. As had become her habit, she had spent an extra couple of hours in the babies' nursery. Two had already been fostered, with a view to full adoption once all the paperwork had been processed, but a newborn had been admitted, sadly undernourished and displaying all the signs of fetal alcohol syndrome.

It broke her heart to think that a child could be abused so poorly, even before birth, and she spent extra time with the wee mite.

She drove back to the castillo slowly, her mind on the children she'd just been with and the prospect of a child of her own. That it would satisfy Alex was a given, but what of the child? Would Alex even be able to spend any time with the baby? He already worked excessively long hours. So much so that since their return they'd barely seen one another, let alone shared a bed.

Was that to be the tenor of their marriage? Passionate couplings to bring forth an heir and nothing in between?

It wasn't what she'd expected of marriage. As difficult as her parents' relationship had been, they had truly loved each other at the beginning. And even when it started to fall apart and the arguments began, they'd been together until her mother—in a fit of pique at her husband—had taken things a step too far with a mutual friend and had betrayed her marriage vows.

Naomi had admitted to Loren, when she'd been about twenty, that she'd regretted forcing Loren's father's hand to divorce her that way, but she hadn't seen any other way out. He'd insisted he still loved her, a fact Loren truly believed, but for Naomi that love had sputtered and died like a guttered candle in the face of the arguments that had become habitual between them.

Loren felt a sharp ache in her chest at the memories, still vivid, of frozen silences between her parents. Silences that would be periodically broken by vicious arguments late into the night when she was supposed to be sleeping.

She'd been about ten years old the first time she became aware of how contentious her parents' marriage had become. Back then she'd hidden under her bedcovers until things had grown silent. By the time she was in her teens she'd sit at the top of the stairs and listen as they threw accusations back and forth.

She could still hear every venomous word of the final exchange that had led to the divorce—of her mother's admission of infidelity, of her father's sobs later after her mother had withdrawn to bed.

Loren swallowed against the sudden lump in her throat and blinked back burning tears. She didn't want that for her child or children. In all conscience she could not bring a child into an unhappy and unstable relationship right from the very start.

But she'd agreed to give Alex the heir he'd stipulated in the prenup. She was honor bound to do so. It was a difficult predicament she found herself in—especially when she wanted so much more.

Only a week ago she'd almost begun to believe her husband might even be beginning to share her feelings for him. That he might be starting to fall a little in love with her, too. But the cold distance he'd maintained since their return had dashed her hopes.

Suddenly the prospect of returning to the castillo held no appeal. She pulled over to the shoulder of the road, then executed a U-turn and headed back in the direction of Puerto Seguro. She needed to be around other people, people who didn't have an agenda as far as she was concerned.

Alex looked up from his seat at the head of the boardroom table in Rey's offices, where he'd arranged to meet with potential investors today. As Giselle approached, he was relieved to see the folder he'd requested from Loren in his PA's hand. A burst of gratitude toward his wife filled him, accompanied by a deep sense of regret that he hadn't been able to spend more time with her lately. He missed her and their nights together with a physical ache, but the negotiations he was in the process of finalizing were vitally important and required all of his attention. Besides, he'd decided it would be selfish to wake her when he arrived home every night after midnight. Alex silently resolved to make it up to Loren once the deal was signed.

Giselle sidled up next to him, one breast brushing not so subtly against his shoulder as she leaned across and put the folder in front of him. There was a time when her actions might have been welcome. That time was well past. He drew away from her touch and noted the tiny crease on her forehead as her brows pulled together in a silent query.

"That will be all, thank you, Giselle."

"All?" She smiled, giving him the sloe-eyed look he'd once found so attractive. "Well, if you're quite sure…"

"Absolutely certain. I am a married man. I shouldn't have to remind you of that."

A married man who'd been neglecting his duties to his wife shamefully. His conscience pricked again.

"Loren looked a little peaked today," Giselle remarked nonchalantly as she finally moved away from his side.

A sudden swell of concern surged through him. "Peaked?" he asked. "What makes you say that?"

"She had a bit of a turn when she brought the papers in from the castillo. Perhaps you've been keeping her up a little too late at night. After all, as we both know, a man of your appetites—"

"That's quite enough," Alex interrupted before she could finish her sentence.

"I was only saying. Anyway, she told me she hadn't eaten breakfast this morning but I couldn't help but wonder if a little del Castillo isn't already making his presence felt. You did want her pregnant, didn't you?"

Pregnant? It was most definitely what he wanted.

The possibility that Giselle spoke the truth bloomed

in his mind, overtaking rational thought. Loren, pregnant with his child? All legalities and legends aside, he hadn't given enough credence to how he'd feel when such an event became a reality. The prospect that his son or daughter could even now be growing in Loren's womb caused an unexpected tightness to coil around his heart. A tightness intermingled with an overwhelming urge to discard his responsibilities to his business and race to Loren's side. To cherish her and share the wonder that they could already be on the way to being parents.

Alex gathered his thoughts together. Despite what his heart wanted, he had duties to fulfill, no matter how inconvenient to him. He looked up and found Giselle watching him carefully, as if waiting for him to confirm or deny her suspicions.

"That would be a matter between my wife and myself. You can head back to the office now, Giselle," he said with finality and looked pointedly at the door.

Giselle made her way out of the boardroom, but her words had left their mark upon him. Try as he might, Alex couldn't ignore his resentment toward the matters of business that had kept him from home so late each night, and that were now an unwelcome barrier between him and the answers he so desperately wanted from his wife.

Loren couldn't say what had drawn her to the graveyard afterward. She'd gone to the city with the determination to lose herself in some shopping, perhaps a meal out, and then to return to the castillo much later. But somehow she'd found herself driving toward the old church on the coast, with its eclectic mix of centuries-old headstones blended with those of more modern times in the burial grounds.

Locking her car in the car park, she pushed through the old wooden gate and picked her way through the headstones until she reached the Dubois family plot. It wasn't difficult to find her father's grave. The stone was the newest and brightest marble amongst the others. Loren knelt down in the grass surrounding the grave and cleared a few of the weeds that had pushed through around the base of his headstone.

"Oh, Papa, did you ever imagine what would come from the pact you and Raphael made all those years ago?" she said, a sudden gust of wind snatching her words and casting them away.

She still missed him so much. By the time her mother had imparted the news that Francois had died of complications after a bout of pneumonia, he'd already been buried. Loren had never had a chance to say goodbye.

The last time she'd spoken to him, though, on one of his frequent phone calls, he'd made her reiterate the one promise he'd asked of her when she'd left Isla Sagrado. Even now she could hear the deep baritone of his voice as he'd spoken across the long-distance telephone lines.

"*Loren,* mi hija, *you must always follow the truth of your heart. Always. Promise me.*"

"Yes, Papa, I promise." Loren now spoke the words out loud. "But it's not so easy when the man of my heart does not feel the same way toward me."

She closed her eyes and bent her head, willing some of her father's wisdom and love to help her with her decision. Did she accept that she had to fulfill the conditions of the prenup, or did she tell Alex she refused to give him the child he had asked for?

Follow the truth of her heart. What was that truth

anymore? All her life she'd believed in one thing, that she was Alex's mate for life. She now accepted how naive that had been. The problem was that truth—her love for Alex—had not diminished. Yes, it had changed. It had grown from childish adoration and infatuation to something she knew was as intrinsic to her being as air was necessary for her to breathe.

So what now, she wondered. Did she accept a marriage as hollow and barren as her parents' marriage had become, or did she fight for what she wanted—what she was due as Alex's wife?

Loren kissed her fingertips and touched them to her father's headstone.

"I love you, Papa. I always will."

Never stop. His automatic response to her words echoed in her heart.

Never stop. Never give up.

And suddenly it was clear what she had to do. If she wanted her husband to *be* her husband, she had to fight for him. Had to fight for what was her right as his partner and as the potential mother of his children. Surely it would not be too much to expect of him that he remain faithful to her, especially not when they were already so obviously compatible. If she could only persuade him to give them a chance, she knew they could make their marriage work.

She straightened up onto her feet and squared her shoulders before resolutely walking back to the car. She would lay her demands on the table to her husband tonight. One way or another, she would have her answer.

And if that answer is no, a small voice in the back of her mind questioned, *what then?*

Loren shook her head as if she could dislodge the

thought before it took hold. She couldn't afford to fail in this. Not when her heart's truth was on the line.

Back at the castillo, Loren was pleased to hear from the housekeeper that Alex would be dining with her and *Abuelo* that evening; in fact, both his brothers would also be there. Knowing that time with his brothers was bound to put Alex in a good mood put a spring in her step as she ascended the stairs to their suite.

And she would make an extra effort with her appearance tonight. Somehow she knew she'd need all the additional armor she could gather around her. She looked at her wristwatch. Yes, she had plenty of time to prepare for the night's success.

In her room, she searched out the candles that had so romantically lit the atmosphere on her disastrous wedding night. She wanted to recreate that golden glow of hope when she and Alex retired to their rooms after dinner. Then she'd show her husband, with her words and with her body, what she expected of him and their marriage.

Satisfied with the placement of the candles, Loren spent a good half hour choosing what to wear for the evening. She didn't want to be too obviously seductive, after all she had a dinner to attend with the four del Castillo men before she would even have so much as an opportunity to have her husband alone. Eventually, she decided upon a simple strapless white gown that skimmed to her knees with flirtatious layers of organza. The bodice was slightly gathered, the scalloped top edge giving a soft and feminine line, while the boned built-in corset meant she could get away with the bare minimum of underwear.

She smiled, remembering her lack of underwear on their honeymoon. It was ironic that even though she'd

bought replacement garments on the first day after
their arrival, once she and Alex had consummated their
marriage she'd had very little need, or opportunity, to
wear any.

The fact that the physical side of their marriage had
stopped upon their return meant that the memory left
a bittersweet taste in her mouth. She pushed the niggle
of doubt about her success for tonight to the very back
of her mind.

She decided to team the dress with an elegant pair
of gold high-heeled pumps and chose a pair of ruby
drop earrings that *Abuelo* had given her on their return
from their honeymoon. Given the style and shape of the
stones, she believed they were probably equally as old
as the heirloom engagement ring she wore on her ring
finger. They'd be the perfect complement to the gown.
A light cobwebby gold shawl to cover her shoulders was
the perfect finishing touch.

Her spirits bolstered, she ran herself a deliciously
deep bubble bath and set about her preparations.

As she had been the first time she'd descended the
stairs alone at the castillo, Loren was aware of the
murmur of male voices from the salon off the main
entrance hall. And uncannily, as she had that very first
time, she felt the weight of generations of del Castillo
brides settle upon her shoulders. She knew, historically,
that most marriages in the del Castillo family in the
past had been structured to gain both political and
financial advantage. Even Alex's parents' marriage
had brought with it the alliance between his mother's
family's vineyards and winery that formed part of the
del Castillo brand today. They had, by the time of their
marriage, been very truly in love, but they had also been

not unaware of the advantages of their union. A union that in all likelihood would not have taken place if the financial gains had not been there in the first place.

That her marriage had been predestined was a fact of life in a family such as this. But a marriage based solely on duty and honor would not be enough to satisfy her. Tonight would establish whether she would finally be able to achieve the kind of marriage she wanted.

A frisson of something cold trickled down her spine and she increased her pace to get to the salon, suddenly eager to see her husband.

She slowed her steps as she drew nearer the salon. Unseemly haste would spoil the image of sensual elegance she'd worked so hard to create tonight. She paused in front of a massive gilt-edged mirror just outside the salon and checked that the somewhat austere hairdo she'd finally settled on, knowing how much Alex loved to tug it loose, remained intact.

Her hand stilled in the air as she heard her husband's voice raised with a thread of anger in it.

"Don't be a fool, Reynard. Marriage is a serious business. I know we all agreed to do our part but I can tell you up front that I regret having done what I have. In fact, I think I may have made the biggest mistake of my life."

Cold shock settled like ice in the pit of Loren's stomach.

"We all know Reynard won't go ahead with actually marrying this girl. The engagement is merely a front to keep *Abuelo* happy as we all agreed." Benedict's voice filtered through the air. "But you needn't worry that I plan on doing anything so stupid as marrying someone I don't love."

"No, we all know you'd marry your car if you

could," Reynard jeered. "I pity the poor woman you do eventually settle down with."

"Well, I pity Loren," Benedict continued. "She didn't ask for any of this."

Loren felt her knees grow weak, her legs unstable beneath her. She had to move, had to get out of there before one of them realized she'd overheard their discussion.

She forced her feet to carry her to immediate refuge in a downstairs guest bathroom and locked the door firmly behind her. Not daring to let go of the breath she was holding in so tight she thought her lungs might burst, she gripped the scallop-shaped marble pedestal basin. Right now it was the only thing keeping her vertical. She was afraid if she let go that she'd sink to the ground and never want to get up again.

The biggest mistake of my life.

Alex's words echoed, over and over, in her mind. Was that how he saw her? Saw their marriage? On the heels of the hope and determination she'd returned home with today, his words were like a death knell to her dreams.

Black spots danced before her eyes and a roaring sound rushed through her head. She forced herself to let go of the breath she'd been holding and dragged in a new breath. The spots began to recede but the pain in her heart only grew with her every inhalation.

Biggest mistake. Biggest mistake.

That she had his brothers' pity was no salve to her wounded soul. She couldn't bear to be the object of any man's pity. Not when all she wanted was Alex's love.

Somehow she had to gather the courage to go in there and face him.

Loren twisted the cold tap on and let the cool water

run over her wrists. As she did so an all-too-familiar ache started in the pit of her belly. An ache that always functioned as a precursor to her period.

Hot tears sprang to her eyes as she realized her fears that she might have been pregnant, and her concerns about Alex's presence as a father, were far outweighed by her desire to have had a part of Alex that would be her own.

She dried off her hands quickly. As she did so, the overhead light caught the bloodred of her ruby engagement ring, the color uncannily symbolic of the end of her expectations.

Alex looked up as Loren joined them in the salon. He allowed a small frown to crease his forehead. He'd expected her much earlier. Mind you, given the slant of the conversation he and his brothers had indulged in, it was just as well she was a little tardy. Reynard's announcement that he'd asked some stranger to be his wife had momentarily knocked his judgment for a loop. It was lucky that Loren had not interrupted their discussion of Rey's news.

She looked beautiful tonight, almost bridal, and for the umpteenth time this week he rued that work had kept him away from her. He'd become quite addicted to his wife in their time in Dubrovnik. Addicted in ways he'd never imagined.

Leaving her to sleep alone in her bed each night after he'd crawled in from working late had been hell, but he was conscious of the need to ensure she remained well. Replenishing the rest she'd missed during their sojourn was one way of doing that.

A flood of heat hit his groin as he remembered the highlights of that sojourn. Right now he wanted to do nothing more than lead her from the salon and take her back upstairs to their suite and into bed. It seemed it was about the only place they could be honest with one another.

Honest? He cringed internally. Their marriage hadn't started with much honesty. But that was something he was now very keen to put right. While it was true he still wanted the heir he'd demanded of her, he wanted so much more besides. And he wanted to give more, too.

He had not only made the biggest mistake of his life in marrying Loren the way he had, he'd done her a major disservice. She deserved to be cherished, to be loved.

The taste of what their marriage could be had made him hungry for more. More of what made a union real and binding.

A union based on love.

His fingers curled tight around the base of his glass as he finally acknowledged his feelings toward his wife. He loved her. Now all he had to do was convince her of the fact. He crossed the room toward her and dropped a kiss to her cool lips. Instantly he was enveloped in the subtle fragrance she used as her signature perfume. Inhaling her scent made him rock hard in seconds.

"I've missed you this week," he said.

"You've been busy. I understand."

Her response wasn't what he'd hoped for. Where was the passionate, teasing lover he'd come to enjoy so much while they were away?

"You're more understanding than most wives, I'll wager."

"But then I'm not *most wives,* am I?"

Her cryptic answer made him study her face more

carefully. She was pale beneath her makeup and there were fine lines of tension about her eyes.

Since their return home, the hope that they'd made a child together during their honeymoon had burned inside of him. That Loren looked somewhat frail this evening gave a hint of truth to the bombshell Giselle had dropped on him this afternoon and made him want to ask Loren outright if she was expecting his baby.

He'd played Giselle's words over in his mind again and again ever since she'd told him about Loren's dizzy spell at the office earlier today. Through all the meetings this afternoon and the interminable legal jargon he'd been forced to wade through, he'd had to fight to keep his focus on the business at hand.

Now that focus was very firmly on the woman before him. His wife. The woman he loved. The woman who now, hopefully, carried their child.

"Are you feeling all right?" he asked, searching her eyes for any hint of a lie.

He raised a hand to her chin and was surprised when she subtly moved clear of his touch.

"I'm fine."

She dismissed his concern with a brittle smile that didn't fool him for a second. Every instinct in him urged him to gather her up in his arms and take her back upstairs. To tie her to the bed, if necessary, until he knew the truth of what lay behind the fragile exterior she exhibited.

"Loren," Reynard interrupted them, bringing Loren a glass of champagne.

Alex was about to intercept it, to tell his brother she wouldn't be drinking tonight or any night for the next several months, but Loren forestalled him by accepting the drink.

Reynard tipped his glass to hers. "You should congratulate me. I'm engaged."

"Engaged? Really? And who is the lucky lady? I had no idea you were even seeing anyone on a regular basis."

There was a slightly wistful note to her voice that pulled at something in Alex's chest.

"Her name is Sara Woodville. She's a Kiwi girl, actually. You might have heard of her. She was here riding for New Zealand in the equestrian trials we sponsored recently."

"And she'd only been on Isla Sagrado for about five minutes before being snapped up by Reynard," Benedict commented drolly. "You've got to hand it to him, he can sure spot an opportunity."

"Well, at least he didn't wait twenty-five years," Loren said, raising her glass to Reynard. "Congratulations, Rey, I hope the two of you will be very happy."

Alex laughed at her comment along with his brothers, but he sensed the thread of bitterness behind her words even if they didn't.

"Well, we can certainly recommend a lovely spot for a honeymoon, can't we?" Alex said, hooking his arm around Loren's slender waist and drawing her against his side.

She stiffened but didn't immediately pull away.

"Oh, yes, I understand that cottage comes very highly recommended."

Again, that hint of double entendre slid like a stiletto through the air. Loren looked across to where *Abuelo* usually sat.

"Is your grandfather not joining us?" she asked.

"No," Alex responded. "His valet sent down a note to say that he wasn't feeling a hundred percent."

"That's not like him. Should I go and check to make sure he's okay?" Loren offered.

If he hadn't thought she would use the opportunity as an excuse to get away from him he would have encouraged her to go. Instead, given how distant she'd been since her arrival this evening, he feared she'd use the visit to his grandfather's rooms as a reason to stay with the old man and not to return—and right now he wanted her here, by his side.

"That won't be necessary. Javier is quite capable of seeing to his needs. Besides, you know how much *Abuelo* hates to be fussed over."

"By you perhaps, but he's never turned away a pretty face—especially Loren's," Benedict noted.

"Be that as it may, Loren can grace us with her company tonight instead. After all, it's the first evening I've had home with her all week."

"Well, don't think you won't have to share her with us. Surely the honeymoon is over by now," Reynard said with a smile designed to needle his older brother even as he hooked an arm in Loren's and drew her away to one side. "Please tell me you are tired of my brother's attentions and we can have our old Loren back again."

Loren laughed, a genuine sound that sent a thrill of longing through Alex. Something untamed knotted deep inside. Logically he knew that his brother was only teasing him, doing what brothers do best when it comes to yanking one another's chain, but he suddenly wished they lived in older times. Times where he could realistically secure Loren away in the castillo's tower rooms and force her to remain only unto him.

He had no doubt that if he answered his instincts and lay claim to her here and now by dragging her from Reynard's clasp that she would find nothing about the action appealing. Besides, forcing her into anything wasn't what he really desired. Truth be told, he simply wanted to hear her laugh—and, more importantly, to be the one who caused her such joy.

Envy didn't sit comfortably on Alex's shoulders. If anything he was the one whose life was coveted by others. That said, he would find some way to remind Reynard of his place.

"Tell us about your new fiancée, Sara, and why you didn't bring her along to meet us this evening," he said pointedly. "Worried she might take one look and decide she's chosen the wrong brother?"

And so the evening rolled on. By the time they took to the massive dining table, with each of the chairs ornately carved with the del Castillo family crest, Alex had firmly reasserted his dominance over his younger siblings. His dominance over his new wife, however, was another matter entirely. She wouldn't so much as meet his eyes and the knowledge definitely set his teeth on edge.

They had just finished their desserts and Reynard was discussing a new publicity drive for the vineyard with Benedict when the castillo's majordomo all but ran into the room. Alex was up and out of his chair before the man came to a halt.

"Qué pasa?" Alex demanded.

"It is *Señor* Aston, he is very ill. Javier, he asks for your help."

"Call for the doctor and an ambulance at once!" Alex barked.

"Already done, *señor.*"

An elevator had been installed for *Abuelo* after his stroke when he'd refused to relocate to a suite downstairs, but Alex eschewed it in favor of the stairs that led to the old man's suite. His grandfather's words, insisting he'd die in the rooms he'd always lived in before anyone could convince him to move, rang loud and clear in Alex's ears. Suddenly the prospect that the elderly head of their family could possibly fulfill that prophecy was frighteningly real.

When Alex arrived in his grandfather's room he was shocked to find the old man lying on the floor, propped up by his manservant and covered with the coverlet from his bed. There was a gray tinge to his features and the muscles on the already weakened side of his face sagged more than usual.

"What happened?" he asked as he knelt to take his grandfather's hand. To feel for himself that the old man's lifeblood still flowed through his body.

"He said he had a headache and preferred to take his evening meal here in his rooms. When I came to take his tray away I found him here, on the floor. I called the doctor straight away and asked Armando to let you know."

Alex heard his brothers enter the room behind him.

"Should we move him onto the bed?" Reynard asked, kneeling down next to Alex.

"No, he is comfortable for now. We'll wait for the doctor and see what he recommends."

Alex felt his grandfather's fingers curl in his, the gnarled digits nowhere near as strong as they should have been. He leaned forward and murmured in Spanish.

"Relax, *Abuelo,* the doctor is coming."

But the old man struggled against him, tugging on Alex's hand as much as he was able. Alex bent closer, trying to make sense of the garbled words coming from his grandfather's mouth. His skin prickled with an icy chill as he finally understood what the old man was saying.

"It is the governess. She was here. It is the curse."

Eleven

"What's he saying?" Benedict asked.

"Nothing," Alex replied, his answer clipped. "He's rambling."

It was always the damn curse. Even now his grandfather wouldn't let go of it. Anger and frustration warred with concern for the old man. He'd done everything he could to put *Abuelo's* mind at ease. He'd married Loren. He believed she was now carrying his baby. But without conclusive proof she was pregnant he couldn't divulge that information to his grandfather.

Or could he? It might be the difference between the old man fighting what appeared to be another stroke or giving up entirely.

Alex gripped his grandfather's hand more tightly. Willing his strength into the old man's failing body.

"It is too late," Aston said, his voice growing weaker. "She has won, hasn't she, the governess?"

"No, *Abuelo,* she hasn't won. The curse, it is broken." Alex forced the words from his lips, prepared to do anything to hold his grandfather to the world around them for as long as he could.

"Broken? Are you certain?" Aston del Castillo's voice grew ever so slightly stronger.

"*Sí,* I am certain."

Just then the doctor arrived at the door, followed closely behind by an emergency paramedic team. In the subsequent bustle of activity as Aston was checked and deemed safe to move to the waiting ambulance downstairs, Alex noticed Loren hovering just inside the doorway.

How long had she been there? Had she heard the exchange between him and his grandfather? No, probably not, he consoled himself. Even Reynard and Benedict who had been at his side could barely hear his grandfather's words.

He looked at her again, studied her drawn features, the concern painted so starkly in her eyes and he knew that she would give him the answer he sought tonight.

"*Señor* del Castillo?"

Alex and his brothers all turned toward the doctor.

"I believe your grandfather has suffered another stroke. I will admit him to hospital immediately. We will need to do a CT scan and possibly an MRI as soon as possible."

"Whatever it takes, Doctor," Alex said, his voice suddenly thick with emotion. "Just make sure he can come back home again."

"We will do everything in our power. I will travel in the ambulance with your grandfather. Perhaps one of you could follow in my car?"

"We will all come to the hospital," Reynard said.

Alex cast Loren a glance. In response she gave a small nod.

"Fine," he said. "Loren and I will bring one of the estate cars and you and Benedict can travel in the doctor's vehicle. That way we all have transport back home."

He could see that Loren wanted to protest, perhaps even to suggest that she'd travel with Reynard or Benedict, but thankfully she merely acceded to his suggestion.

They completed the drive to the hospital, on the outskirts of Puerto Seguro, in silence. Alex had no need for casual conversation when all he wanted right now was to see his grandfather safely settled in the hospital and to hear a promising prognosis for his future from the neurological specialist on call.

They were pulling up outside the hospital when he placed a hand on Loren's arm and squeezed lightly.

"Thank you," he said.

"What for? I've done nothing tonight."

"For coming with me."

He meant it, too. It would reassure his grandfather to see Loren with him. Would help underline his promise that the curse was well and truly broken. That there was a power of hope ahead for the del Castillo family.

"Alex, you know I would do anything for your grandfather."

Anything for his grandfather but not for him? Alex bit back the question before he could give it voice.

"I am grateful for that," he finally managed through a throat that had suddenly grown thick with emotion.

"He's strong, Alex. He'll be okay."

Loren placed her free hand over his and pressed

firmly, as if trying to underline her words and make them a reality.

He could only nod. Drawing in a deep breath, he pulled away from her, missing the contact instantly.

"Come, let's go into the emergency department."

He helped her from the car and was relieved when she didn't pull away from him as he draped one arm around her shoulders and pulled her close against his side. Where she belonged, he reminded himself. No matter what this strange distant game she had played tonight, she was his wife and she belonged with him. Always.

It was nearly two in the morning when they made it back to the castillo. Alex's grandfather was comfortably settled in a private room at the hospital, his neurologist hopeful that because of Javier's quick call for help that they had been successful in halting any additional damage as a result of the ischemic stroke he'd suffered. They'd been able to medicate as soon as the scan results had confirmed their suspicions, falling just within the window of time vital to ensure a strong chance of survival and recovery.

Alex had taken a moment to thank Javier as they'd arrived home. The manservant had been awaiting their arrival and broke into unashamed sobs of relief when given the news that his master would in all likelihood pull through with minimal permanent damage.

Reynard and Benedict had chosen to take taxis to their homes directly from the hospital, rather than return to the castillo for their vehicles or stay over at their old family home. The next day would be soon enough to work out the logistics of recovering their vehicles. Besides, they would undoubtedly cross over with one another at the hospital as each planned to be there with their grandfather for as much time as their work commitments permitted.

Loren left Alex with Javier and went up the stairs to their rooms, feeling more than twice her age as she let herself into her bedroom and kicked off her shoes.

She looked around the room, feeling as if it had been days since she'd been here, rather than the hours it had actually been. Her eyes fell on the fragrant candles she'd set around the room in an effort to create the right atmosphere in which to seduce her husband. A seduction she'd planned before she'd heard what she suspected was the first excruciating shred of complete honesty from him in all her time back here.

In the drama surrounding *Abuelo's* stroke, the earlier events of the evening had been pushed aside, but now every word she'd overhead came rushing back in a painful remembrance.

She quickly gathered the candles up and dropped them into the wastebasket near her escritoire. She stood there, shaking with anger. How dare he have played with her life like that and then call it a mistake?

"Loren?" Alex spoke from the entrance to her bedroom. "Are you all right?"

A short sharp sound burst from her throat. It should have been a laugh but there was far too much bitterness behind it to even mimic humor. Alex covered the distance toward her and tried to take her in his arms, but she pulled free and took two steps back from him.

"Don't! Don't touch me."

She had to keep some distance between them; it was the only way she could keep her anger in the forefront of her mind when all her body wanted to do was meld with his and find again the ecstasy they'd shared for all too brief a time. She knew it took more than a physical connection to keep a marriage alive.

"Don't touch you? What is wrong? I've barely seen you all week and we've had a very distressing evening. I need to touch you. I need *you*."

"No." She shook her head.

The bleak weariness that had been on Alex's face earlier was now replaced by sharp intellect and a satisfied nod of understanding. "You are emotional. It is only to be expected. Giselle told me today you might be pregnant."

Loren couldn't believe her ears. "Giselle *what?*"

Alex continued, "Don't you think that you should perhaps have given me the news yourself?"

"And when would I have had the opportunity? You've been away from the castillo all week—not even home at night until very late and then gone early in the morning. Even today, on the telephone, you treated me as no more than a private messenger service." She cut the air between them with a sweep of her hand. "Whatever, as it happens, your assistant's conjecture is premature. My cycle was obviously out of sync. Whether it was from the travel or the stress of the wedding, it matters little. Tomorrow I will have my period."

"And you know this for sure because?" he growled.

"Because I know my own body, and I know I'm not pregnant."

Alex blew out a breath and closed his eyes, his features suddenly contorted with disappointment. When he opened his eyes she was struck by the raw regret mirrored there. She decided to ignore it. She was no doubt as wrong about his feelings on this as she'd been about so many things to do with Alexander del Castillo.

If he had any regrets it would only be that he had to continue with this total charade of a marriage to get the heir he so desperately wanted.

"I've given the matter of our prenuptial agreement further thought," she continued. "I believe it would be best for us to go back to my original request for an assisted pregnancy. In fact, I'd prefer it."

"Prefer it?" Alex echoed.

"Yes. Intercourse between us is clearly going to be a hit-and-miss affair. After all, it's not as if we didn't try hard enough before. To be honest with you, I'm not keen to resume that side of our marriage."

"Not keen." His voice was flat, his jaw rock hard.

She clenched her hands into fists at her sides, her fingernails digging small crescents.

"That's right. Plus, I believe you also wish to get on with things yourself."

"Things? Would you care to define exactly what those things are?"

Loren chewed her lower lip for a second. Did she dare acknowledge that she knew of his affair with Giselle, that she was aware he'd been biding his time to pick up again where they'd left off? She lifted her chin and met his gaze squarely.

"I think you know what I'm referring to. We both know this marriage between us was a mistake. In fact I heard you say the very thing yourself tonight."

"You heard me say that?" His voice was deadpan, as was the expression in his eyes.

Alex stepped in closer, filling her senses with his presence. Loren stood her ground. He knew very well what he'd said and now he knew she'd overheard him.

"Alex, as I said before, I will fulfill my duties to you under our legal agreement. That means I must deliver you a child. There was nothing in there about how I am to achieve that goal so I elect to use the clinical facility here on the island. Now, if that is all, it has been an extremely long and demanding day and I would like to get some sleep."

"There was also nothing in there about you being the one to elect how you should fall pregnant," Alex said.

Loren felt her heart stutter in her chest before resuming a rapid rhythm. "Are you suggesting you would force me?"

"Force? No, I doubt that would be necessary. Not when I know I can do this and have you willing in my arms."

He snaked one arm around her waist and drew her against his body, molding her hips to his lower body, widening his stance to cradle her there. Instantly Loren felt the answering call of her body to his, the intensity of awareness, the heated flow of blood through her veins.

When Alex bent his head to hers and caught her lips in a possessive kiss she found herself answering in kind. Allowing her anger an outlet, showing him he may be able to dominate her physically but he would never dominate her will.

They were both panting, their breathing discordant and harsh in the air between them, when Alex broke away.

"Out of respect for your oncoming *condition*," he said, his fingers splaying across her hip and lower belly, "I will not continue, but I believe my point has been made. You cannot refuse me, Loren. Your own body makes a lie of that."

As she watched him leave the bedroom and pull her door closed behind him she forced herself to acknowledge he was painfully right. She'd adored him as a child, been infatuated with him as a teen. Now she loved him with every cell in her body as a woman. Even knowing he would still choose another did not assuage the loss she felt as he'd walked away.

Was this how her father had felt when he'd learned of her mother's infidelity? This frantic sense of hurt and betrayal, the urgent desire to turn back the clock and start over—to get things right next time?

Her mother had once, and only once, alluded to the fact that she'd chosen to do something totally against her nature to force her husband to finally let her go. That the passionate highs and desperate lows of their rocky marriage had been as destructive as they'd been exhilarating and that she'd been incapable of bearing them any longer.

The fact that Naomi had been unfaithful to Francois Dubois to break free of her marriage had been a cop-out as far as Loren was concerned. She'd always believed that if they had loved one another enough they could have made things work. Not all marriages were always sailed on an even keel. Some people, some relationships, were just not cut out to be like that. That didn't mean they had to fall apart.

But the one thing Loren did know for certain was that when one partner loved less, or not at all, that marriage was doomed to failure.

When Loren woke the next morning with her period she was torn between relief that she wasn't yet forced to bring a baby into a loveless marriage and sorrow that the intimacy they'd shared in so much happier times, no matter how orchestrated, had not resulted in a child to love. After taking care of her needs she carried on through into the sitting room of their suite. Her maid usually ensured a tray was sent up for Loren each morning with her preference of cereal and yogurt for breakfast together with freshly squeezed orange juice. Loren usually took this quiet time in the morning to review the papers and plan her day.

She was surprised, however, to see Alex pacing the carpet when she pushed open her chamber door.

"*Abuelo?*" she asked, one hand to her throat. "Is everything all right?"

"*Sí,* he is resting comfortably. That is not why I'm here."

"Oh? What is it, then?" Loren went instantly on the defensive. "Ready to go for round two in the baby debate?"

"There is no debate," Alex responded, his voice harsh.

"Well, there certainly is no debate today. I have my period. You can go and carry on with whatever it is you're supposed to be doing today."

"Are you certain?"

Loren just stared at him. She knew she looked anything but her usual self this morning. The cramps had started in earnest shortly after she'd gone to bed and had kept her awake for the rest of the night. Her reflection in the mirror had shown her cheeks were pale, her eyes dark and shadowed.

"I will contact the doctor today and find out what is necessary to instigate the procedure."

Alex rubbed one hand across his eyes and sighed.

"Loren, it doesn't have to be like this."

"Yes, Alex, it does. We wouldn't want there to be any further *mistakes,* now would we?"

"You have taken my words out of context," he argued back.

"Just how out of context?"

Alex felt a swirl of helplessness eddy within him in the growing whirlpool of frustration he'd been feeling since the previous night. If only he could convince her to listen to what he'd really meant. Caution warned him that today was probably not the best time to broach the subject of his innermost thoughts. She was unlikely to believe him if he declared his love for her right now, and given how he'd dissembled to her already he could hardly blame her.

Just seeing her like this, looking bruised and fragile, made him want to sweep her into his arms and tuck her back into her bed. To force her to relax and regain her strength. To be the vibrant young woman he'd reintroduced himself to in New Zealand.

"I do not wish to banter with you about something as important as this when you are clearly not at your best. Perhaps when you are feeling better and more amenable to discussion—"

"This is not just some passing mood, Alex! I'm serious. As far as I am concerned, until we are discussing the creation of our child, we have nothing else to say to one another."

"Fine," he said in clipped tones, not wanting to acknowledge the hurt her words had inflicted upon his hopes. "You contact the clinic. Let me know when and where I'm needed or if you happen to change your mind from this ridiculous insistence of yours."

Alex drove to his office in a fury, barely even noticing the summer glory of the countryside that led to the resort's location.

The fact Loren was totally unwilling to resume

the physical side of their marriage completely baffled him. They had been perfect together. So she'd overhead him saying he'd made a mistake. He had. He was man enough to admit that. But her adamant refusal to enter into discussions with him unless they were discussing their child caused a pain inside him that was physical as much as it was emotional. A pain he was totally unaccustomed to feeling. If this was love, no wonder his ancestors had primarily chosen to marry for any other reason but that. Anything was better than giving someone else the power to make you hurt inside the way he hurt right now.

He thought fleetingly of the situation that had brought about his marriage to Loren. The governess's curse may not be real, but it had certainly made an impact on his life, and not one he was happy to accede to.

The three supposed edicts of the governess as she'd cursed his ancestor played back in his head—honor, truth and love. Well, he had both honored and continued to love his grandfather, and he'd tried to love his wife. Tried, and failed. It was a failure he wanted to put behind him as quickly and effectively as he could.

As he pressed the accelerator down a little harder, sending his car flying along the resort road, he vowed Loren would come back into his arms, and into his bed, on his terms or no terms at all.

Twelve

It had been two weeks since their last civil conversation beyond the frozen politeness they displayed to everyone at mealtimes at the castillo. At least those mealtimes when Alex deigned to come home.

His grandfather had been moved from the hospital, protestingly, into convalescent care. That he would be allowed back home when he met the rehabilitation markers set by his doctors was of no consolation to him. Loren had spent most of her days divided between keeping him company, preventing him from being cheerfully murdered by the staff at the facility where he was staying and performing her duties at the orphanage.

Each time she held the babies, she ached a little more for the child she did not carry. But, she told herself, that need would soon be assuaged by the procedures she would soon commence. Her doctor had agreed to begin the necessary treatments once both she and Alex were fully apprised of the information relating to them.

Now she finally had all that information to hand and she was determined to start whatever was necessary as soon as possible—which meant ensuring Alex was equally informed.

The prospect of undergoing injections to ensure she produced multiple viable eggs was something she didn't look forward to, but she was prepared to endure whatever she had to. She'd promised, legally and personally, to carry out her end of the agreement. She was her father's daughter. She did not renege on anything.

Loren checked her reflection before grabbing the file of papers the doctor and his nurse had given her. She smoothed her straight dark hair with one hand before straightening her shoulders and giving herself a small nod of approval. She was ready to go to Alex's office.

The dark blue shift she wore tapered to her slender form perfectly, and her matching sling-back shoes confirmed her businesslike appearance. And that's all this was. A business transaction. The execution of a plan.

At the resort, the receptionist waved Loren through to Alex's offices. At his door she paused, her hand curled, knuckles ready to rap on the smooth wooden surface. But then she decided against it. She was his wife, after all. There had to be some advantages to it.

She reached for the polished steel handle, pushed open the door and stepped inside only to come to a rapid halt at the sight before her.

Giselle was all but straddling Alex's lap—her hair a golden tumble down her back, her hand covering his own as it pushed up the hem of her skirt, her other arm draped around his neck and his head bent into the curve of hers.

Loren gave a startled gasp and spun on her heel before stopping and forcing herself to face the couple who were now apart. Giselle quickly stood beside Alex's chair and slowly rearranged her clothing. Her face wore a distinct look of sly satisfaction—Alex's, however, wore one of dark fury.

Loren looked from one to the other, suddenly overwhelmed with a determination that would brook no denial. She would not tolerate this. If Alex wanted a child in this marriage then he'd have to play by her rules and her rules demanded no infidelity.

It was time she grew a spine and fought back. Adrenaline coursed through her body. Suddenly she could begin to understand why people took scary risks. The sense of exhilaration was both terrifying and electrifying at the same time.

She pointed one finger at Giselle. "You. Get out."

"I beg to differ," Giselle drawled. "I believe you're the one out of place here."

"You can beg all you like, but you will be doing it elsewhere from now on. Get out, now, and stay the hell away from my husband."

"Alex!" The other woman appealed to the silent male figure at her side. "You can't let her talk to me like that. You have to tell her about us."

"What's it to be, Alex?" Loren challenged.

"Leave us," he said, his voice calm and level.

"Surely you don't expect me—" Giselle protested.

Loren smiled at her, although it was more a baring of teeth than a signal of pleasure. "I believe my husband asked you to leave."

With a sniff of disdain Giselle collected her bag,

then with a hand trailing the side of Alex's face she said, "Should you change your mind, you know where to reach me."

Loren watched as Giselle sashayed out of the office and went to close the door firmly behind her. Then she crossed back over to Alex's desk and dropped the clinic folder onto his desk in front of him.

"If you want to go ahead and have a baby with me then there have to be some boundaries. The most important is that you keep your hands off other women or you can consider our marriage over."

He gave a short laugh. "Marriage? You think what we have is a marriage?"

"We have what approximates a marriage, but we'll have what is most definitely a divorce if you so much as touch another woman again."

Alex leaned back in his leather executive chair and steepled his fingers. Giselle's move on him had taken him by surprise. He'd made it more than clear, both before he'd traveled to New Zealand and since his return and subsequent marriage to Loren, that anything he and Giselle had shared was well and truly over.

At first she'd been subtle—well, subtle for Giselle anyway. In recent weeks, her overtures had been more blatant, but nothing like today's blitzkrieg. He'd been on the verge of pushing her away—off his lap and out of his employ—when Loren had entered his office. He'd half expected Loren to simply leave again, but even then his little wife had surprised him.

Despite keeping her distance from him it was patently clear she was not prepared to share her toys, either. The knowledge gave him a surge of satisfaction. Perhaps now she would listen to reason.

He reached forward and flicked open the file she'd

dropped on his desk with one finger. His eyes skimmed the first page of details and everything inside him rebelled. No way would he accede to this barbaric coercion of nature when for them, in all likelihood, it was not even necessary.

"No other women, you say?" he asked, arching one brow and allowing his lips to relax into a smile.

"You heard me."

His wife stood opposite him, standing her ground like a sentinel.

"Hmm." Alex pursed his lips in consideration. "Yet you do not plan to share your bed with me like a dutiful wife ought?"

"We've been over this, Alex. You don't love me, yet you want a baby with me. Some people might be able to separate emotion from their physical behavior but I am not one of them. I won't share my bed with you if your only purpose in coming to me is to conceive a child."

There was a tiny break in her voice. A break that gave him the leverage he was looking for. She had not stopped loving him, he was sure of it. And if she hadn't, then he could press home his advantage and use this as an opportunity to win her back. To make their marriage the genuine article.

"I see. Well, then there is nothing for it but for me to agree to your condition that I not touch another woman."

"Thank you," she said, her breath escaping in a rush.

He raised a hand. "I haven't finished. I do agree to your condition, on a condition of my own. I refuse to allow you to submit to this process, Loren. We will conceive our child the old-fashioned way."

"No."

"Then I'm sorry. Because on this I refuse to negotiate."

"And I refuse to take another woman's leavings. Our marriage is over."

Before he could stop her Loren had turned and left his office. Over? Surely she didn't mean it. Shock reverberated through his body. Shock followed rapidly by a determination to stop her in her tracks. To somehow make her retract her statement, to admit her love for him, to allow him to admit his for her. He would not let her go, not like this, not ever. Galvanized by a combination of fear and resolve, he shot from his chair and out of his office.

By the time he reached the reception area he was just in time to see his wife's sleek convertible spin out of the parking lot and up the driveway leading to the main road. He felt his jacket pocket for his keys and cursed that he'd left them in his briefcase instead. There was no time to waste. Alex turned and zeroed in on his receptionist.

"Your car keys, give them to me now."

Flustered, the woman withdrew her handbag from a file drawer and extracted her keys.

"It's the Fiat, at the end of the staff car park," she said with wide eyes.

"*Gracias,* you'll find my keys in the case beside my desk. Take my car tonight."

"The Lamborghini?"

But Alex barely heard her. He had to reach Loren before she did something stupid, like leave him for good.

She could barely see through the tears that spilled from her eyes and down her cheeks as she grabbed clothes indiscriminately from her wardrobe and drawers and jammed them into her suitcase.

Was it so unreasonable to expect him not to have affairs?

Perhaps it was if *she* wasn't prepared to give him the surcease his male body obviously demanded. But what of her needs? What of the pleasures he'd taught her to receive and, in turn, to give? If she didn't have him, she didn't want anybody else and she most definitely wasn't prepared to share him.

Besides, he didn't want *her*. Not really. He only wanted her to create the heir he so desperately needed to provide to prove to *Abuelo* that the curse was nothing but hearsay on the tail of a three-hundred-year-old legend. She certainly had to admire the lengths he was prepared to go to set his grandfather's mind at rest, but the cost wasn't something she was prepared to pay. Not anymore. Not when beneath it all he still thought marrying her had been a mistake.

Loren bit back a sob as she shoved the swimwear and the sarongs she'd taken to Dubrovnik into the case and dashed the tears from her cheeks. A sound behind her made her pause. Before she could return to her task, she was spun around. The articles of clothing she still held were plucked from her hands and cast to the floor at her feet.

Alex stood before her, his strong hands holding her upper arms firmly so she couldn't pull away.

"I am no woman's leavings," he ground out in a harsh breath. "Unless, of course, you really are planning to leave me?"

"Of course I'm leaving you. I can't do this anymore, Alex. I can't."

"Why? Tell me." His fingers curled into her arms, pulling her closer to him.

"I can't share you. I refuse to share you. You know I love you, I always have—stupidly, now more than ever. I accepted when I married you that you didn't love me. I could live with that. But I cannot live with you taking your pleasure from other women. I lived through that with my parents. My mother's infidelity drove them both insane. I will not fall victim to that kind of desperate dependence. Not even for you."

"But you have no need to share me. I have never been unfaithful to you, Loren. Please, believe me."

She yanked herself free from his grasp and a choked laugh erupted from her throat.

"Don't treat me like a fool. From the second I arrived here Giselle has made it perfectly clear that you were only biding time with me until I provided you with an heir. Even you yourself did nothing to disabuse me of that belief."

"And our honeymoon? Did that mean nothing to you?"

"Mean nothing? It meant *everything* to me when we could finally be a couple. Yet the second we returned everything went back to how it was before. Including your relationship with your assistant."

"My relationship with Giselle has been nothing but professional for several months."

"How can you expect me to believe that? All those late nights and early mornings? I never saw you, you never spoke to me. And what about what I interrupted today?"

"I admit, I was involved with Giselle for a short period before I came to New Zealand, but once I'd decided to marry you I broke things off with her. Today was Giselle's desperate attempt to reignite a flame that never went beyond a distant flicker. What we shared was well and truly over before I asked you into my life, Loren. It's only ever been you since then."

Loren just shook her head. She wished she could accept his words as the truth but she hurt too much.

"Why should I believe you, Alex? Why should I believe my husband when he thinks our whole marriage is a mistake?"

"Because I love you!"

"Don't lie to me about that, Alex. Not now, not ever!"

She spun away from him and clutched her arms around her body as if she could somehow assuage the empty pain that filled her chest in the place of her heart and the death of her dreams.

He turned her back to face him and cupped his hands around her face, tilting it up so her eyes would meet his.

"Loren, I love *you*. I didn't plan to. To be totally honest, I didn't even want to. I thought we could marry, and that our feelings for each other would never go beyond companionship at best. How wrong I was!" He shook his head at his own foolishness. "I didn't count on falling in love with you, but from the moment you stood up to your mother, you started to inveigle your way into my heart. Day by day, week by week, I've learned to respect you and to love you.

"That's what I meant when I told my brothers I had made a mistake marrying you the way I had. It was wrong to rush into marriage merely to disprove some stupid curse that has no bearing on our lives today no matter what my grandfather believes. It was wrong to use you that way. But I do not regret marrying you, Loren.

I will never regret that. If I had this time over again I would still have brought you back to Isla Sagrado, back home, but I would have taken the time to woo you, to learn about the woman you are now, to acknowledge that love is not something to be spurned or used to a man's advantage." He pressed a kiss to her forehead. "Loren, please, give me another chance. Give *us* another chance."

Confusion swirled inside her. Half of her wanted to believe him, to have faith in his words and hold them to her forever. But the other half still hurt, deeply and most painfully. Her trust in him had been broken, her pride dashed. Deep down, she didn't want to lay herself open for any more hurt.

"I don't know if I can," she whispered. "I don't know if I even want to try again."

His dark eyes deepened to darkest black as she saw her own pain reflected in their depths.

"Then go. Return to New Zealand. I will not hold you to a marriage that you no longer can commit to. I will see to our dissolution, to your freedom. I'm sorry, Loren. I never thought things would come to this. As much as it breaks my heart, I would rather see you free to go than be trapped here with me, even as much as I need you by my side."

"You would do that? You'd let me just leave? What about the curse? What about *Abuelo?*"

"Don't you understand? Without your love, without you, I will forever be cursed. If you cannot love me then who am I to hold you here? I can only beg your forgiveness for being such a fool and for using you the way I did.

"Losing you has taught me a valuable life lesson. There is more to honoring a parent's wish and a family's expectations than just going through the motions. Without love, it means nothing."

He let her go and Loren rocked slightly on her feet as he did so. The confusion that had so clouded her mind only moments ago began to solidify into one clear thought.

Alexander del Castillo loved her.

Finally, this tall, proud man was hers.

Relief coursed through her veins followed by a bubbling rush of exhilaration. She drew in a deep breath.

"Alex," she said, in as level a tone as she could manage, "would you do one final thing for me?"

"Anything."

"Would you bring my suitcase?"

She saw his features settle into a frozen mask, but to his credit he said nothing. Merely zipped up the case and hefted it off the bed with one hand.

"Thank you," she said, and started walking through their suite and into his bed chamber.

"What are you doing?" he asked, his voice thick as if his throat was constricted.

"I don't want to be apart from you anymore—not even in separate rooms."

"Then you're staying?"

"You couldn't get rid of me now for anything."

Loren looked at him now, face-to-face, surprised to see the sheen of tears reflected in his eyes. That this powerful man was reduced to tears by the fact that she'd chosen to remain with him said it all.

"Love me, Alex."

"Forever, *mi querida*."

His arms closed around her, making her feel as if she'd finally come home. After their clothing had been torn from their bodies and they came together on his massive pedestal bed Loren knew she was home forever.

Past hurts dissolved into distant memories as his hands caressed her body with a new reverence. Fears about the future disappeared as she welcomed him inside her, not only physically but, finally, wholly and emotionally, as well.

It was late and the castillo silent and brooding in the darkness as Alex led Loren down the stairs.

"Where are you taking me?" Loren asked in a whisper.

"There is one more thing we need to do. Trust me."

He felt his heart swell as her slender fingers tightened in his. That small silent communication meant so much. To finally have her trust and to know he honestly returned it was one of the greatest gifts he'd ever received.

Their slippered feet made no sound as they crossed the great hall toward the small private chapel that formed part of the castillo's ancient history. The well-tended chapel door swung open silently beneath his touch.

"Wait here a moment," he instructed before moving swiftly down the center aisle of the centuries-old place of worship.

Moonlight gave eerie illumination to the stained-glass windows that had been fitted by successive generations of del Castillos. At the altar Alex lit the thick candles in their squat candelabra, letting their golden glow chase the shadows of the past to the corners of the chapel.

He turned back to Loren, covering the short distance

back to the door, to his bride, in seconds. Taking her hand again, he led her to the altar.

"I should have done this right the first time. I owed you that," he said, stroking the side of her face softly before letting his hands reach down to take both of hers in his own.

"It's all right, Alex. We survived anyway."

Her smile was bittersweet and Alex made a silent vow to ensure that the last of their ghosts were banished from this moment.

"We may have survived but you deserve more than that. This time I don't want there to be any doubt.

"Loren, I love you for your strength in the face of adversity, for your pride and incredible sense of honor and for the gift of your love to me, even when I didn't deserve it. From this day forward, you will never again be lonely for I will always be at your side to give you comfort and to support you in whatever you do for all of our lives together.

"I promise you, I will always be your rock, I will always honor you, remain true only to you and I will always love you—today and forever."

He lifted her hand and placed a kiss on her ring finger, sealing a brand upon her skin where his rings already claimed her as his by law. He rested their clasped hands against his chest as Loren took a deep breath and started to speak, her voice low and clear in the air between them.

"Alex, I have always loved you for your principles, for your direction and your love for your family. I am honored to be your wife, to be your partner for life and to be the one to support you and love you through whatever comes our way in the future. I treasure your love for me and will always do everything in my power to protect and nurture that love.

"Together I know we can weather any storm and be safe in the knowledge that it will only bring us closer and will only serve to help me love you more. I can't wait to have children with you, to watch them grow with your guidance and strength behind them and I promise that I will always be there for you and always love you."

She reached up and kissed him, sealing their vows to one another with a hunger and a pledge that promised a happier future.

As one, they bent to blow out the candles, then left the chapel to return to their chamber, oblivious to the fading apparition in the far reaches of the shadows—a woman in eighteenth-century dress—smiling.

* * * * *

Don't miss Reynard's story,
STAND-IN BRIDE'S SEDUCTION,
when Yvonne Lindsay's
WED AT ANY PRICE trilogy
continues next month.
On sale September 14, 2010
from Silhouette Desire.

COMING NEXT MONTH

Available October 12, 2010

#2041 ULTIMATUM: MARRIAGE
Ann Major
Man of the Month

#2042 TAMING HER BILLIONAIRE BOSS
Maxine Sullivan
Dynasties: The Jarrods

#2043 CINDERELLA & THE CEO
Maureen Child
Kings of California

#2044 FOR THE SAKE OF THE SECRET CHILD
Yvonne Lindsay
Wed at Any Price

#2045 SAVED BY THE SHEIKH!
Tessa Radley

#2046 FROM BOARDROOM TO WEDDING BED?
Jules Bennett

REQUEST YOUR FREE BOOKS!

2 FREE NOVELS
PLUS 2
FREE GIFTS!

Passionate, Powerful, Provocative!

SDES10R

HARLEQUIN®

A Romance

FOR EVERY MOOD™

Spotlight on
Heart & Home

Heartwarming romances
where love can happen
right when you least expect it.

See the next page to enjoy a sneak peek
from Harlequin Superromance®,
a Heart and Home series.

CATHHHSR10

Enjoy a sneak peek at fan favorite Molly O'Keefe's
Harlequin Superromance miniseries,
THE NOTORIOUS O'NEILLS, *with*
TYLER O'NEILL'S REDEMPTION,
available September 2010
only from Harlequin Superromance.

Police chief Juliette Tremblant recognized the shape of the man strolling down the street—in as calm and leisurely fashion as if it were the middle of the day rather than midnight. She slowed her car, convinced her eyes were playing tricks on her. It had been a long time since Tyler O'Neill had been seen in this town.

As she pulled to a stop at the curb, he turned toward her, and her heart about stopped.

"What the hell are you doing here, Tyler?"

"Well, if it isn't Juliette Tremblant." He made his way over to her, then leaned down so he could look her in the eye. He was close enough to touch.

Juliette was not, repeat, *not* going to touch Tyler O'Neill. Not with her fingers. Not with a ten-foot pole. There would be no touching. Which was too bad, since it was the only way she was ever going to convince herself the man standing in front of her—as rumpled and heart-stoppingly handsome now as he'd been at sixteen—was real.

And not a figment of all her furious revenge dreams.

"What are you doing back in Bonne Terre?" she asked.

"The manor is sitting empty," Tyler said and shrugged, as though his arriving out of the blue after ten years was casual. "Seems like someone should be watching over the family home."

"You?" She laughed at the very notion of him being here for any unselfish reason. "Please."

He stared at her for a second, then smiled. Her heart fluttered against her chest—a small mechanical bird powered by that smile.

"You're right." But that cryptic comment was all he offered.

Juliette bit her lip against the other questions.

Why did you go?

Why didn't you write? Call?

What did I do?

But what would be the point? Ten years of silence were all the answer she really needed.

She had sworn off feeling anything for this man long ago. Yet one look at him and all the old hurt and rage resurfaced as though they'd been waiting for the chance. That made her mad.

She put the car in gear, determined not to waste another minute thinking about Tyler O'Neill. "Have a good night, Tyler," she said, liking all the cool "go screw yourself" she managed to fit into those words.

It seems Juliette has an old score to settle with Tyler.
Pick up TYLER O'NEILL'S REDEMPTION
to see how he makes it up to her.
Available September 2010,
only from Harlequin Superromance.

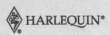

Silhouette® *Desire*

New York Times **and** USA TODAY
bestselling author

BRENDA JACKSON

brings you

WHAT A WESTMORELAND WANTS,

another seductive Westmoreland tale.

Part of the Man of the Month series

Callum is hopeful that once he gets
Gemma Westmoreland on his native turf
he will wine and dine her with a seduction plan
he has been working on for years—one that
guarantees to make her his.

Available September wherever books are sold.

**Look for a new Man of the Month
by other top selling authors each month.**

Always Powerful, Passionate and Provocative.

MARGARET WAY

introduces

THE Rylance DYNASTY

**The lives & loves of
Australia's most powerful family**

Growing up in the spotlight hasn't been easy, but the two
Rylance heirs, Corin and his sister, Zara, have come of age
and are ready to claim their inheritance. Though they are
privileged, proud and powerful, they are about to discover
that there are some things money can't buy....

Look for:

Australia's Most Eligible Bachelor
Available September

Cattle Baron Needs a Bride
Available October

www.eHarlequin.com

HR17679